A RINGSIDE
ROMANCE

LOSING IT
CHRISTINE D'ABO

RIPTIDE
PUBLISHING

Riptide Publishing
PO Box 1537
Burnsville, NC 28714
www.riptidepublishing.com

Losing It

Cover art: L.C. Chase, lcchase.com/design.htm
Editors: Sarah Lyons, May Peterson, maypetersonbooks.com
Layout: L.C. Chase, lcchase.com/design.htm

ISBN: 978-1-62649-699-6

First edition
February, 2018

Also available in ebook:
ISBN: 978-1-62649-698-9

A RINGSIDE ROMANCE

LOSING IT
CHRISTINE D'ABO

RIPTIDE
PUBLISHING

To all of my friends who have helped me keep it together over the past few years.
I love you all.

TABLE OF
CONTENTS

CHAPTER ONE

Justin McCormick flexed his fingers as he stood outside of Ringside Gym. God, this was a terrible idea, but for the first time in his adult life, he was at a complete loss for what else to do. He had no job, his savings were getting dangerously low, and he'd burned more than a few professional bridges over the years while doing his former employer's bidding. That made getting out of this particular mess difficult.

Plus, he was wearing glasses for the first time in years. He *hated* glasses.

He hadn't anticipated needing to start over at this stage in his life. Everything had been going the way he'd wanted; he'd achieved each of his goals in order. And yet . . .

Like vapor, his career and personal life had vanished in a puff of smoke.

The warm air was unusual for this early in April in Toronto, or so the taxi driver had said on the way through traffic. Justin hadn't bothered to respond, not particularly caring about the current state of meteorological affairs. The nice weather wasn't going to make it any easier for him to get a job with a sufficient income to allow him to live in Toronto in the manner that he'd been previously accustomed to. His résumé—which would be the envy of most—hadn't gotten him much, but as far as he could tell, it was his reputation rather than his experience that was holding him back.

The main thing he'd spent a decade cultivating was now a liability. Ironic.

The sidewalk was full of people of all sorts, many of whom were dressed for work, probably rushing off to some important meeting or other. Justin averted his eyes as a man, who appeared to be homeless, started to come toward him. He could feel the other man's gaze on him as he got close, but instead of engaging, Justin stepped toward the window and began to read a notice of a new kickboxing class.

The smell of body odor washed over Justin as the man moved to stand beside him. "Excuse me. Do you have any change?"

"No." Justin didn't bother to mask his gruff nature, and kept his gaze fixed on the poster.

The man nodded and passed Justin. "That's okay. You have a great day."

Justin turned his head and watched him ask a passing woman the same thing. She stepped around him, throwing him a dirty look as she went by. The man waved at her and took up a post a few feet from the gym entrance. Justin did his best to ignore him, but the longer he stood there, the louder his conscience started to yell at him.

Instead he reached into his pocket and took out the three toonies he'd been saving for a coffee. He walked over and held them out. "Here."

"You found some change after all." The man smiled and put it into his pocket. "Thank you."

Justin narrowed his gaze. "I can take it back if you want?"

"It's all good. Much appreciated." He'd moved a few steps away when Justin heard him mutter. "Asshole."

Justin ignored him and went back to the gym door, because what else could he do? He *was* an asshole, though he'd been trying harder in recent months to cull those behaviors. A fresh start, and all that shit. Except that now he was standing in front of the place where his former charge Grady now worked, skulking about like he'd been accused of doing so many times in the past.

This had been a horrible idea. They'd parted on decent terms, but Grady wouldn't want him around now that he'd gotten his own life on track. So, Justin took a breath, turned, and slowly walked past the gym. This wasn't what he needed, to reconnect with Grady and try to rekindle a friendship. No, he needed to find a job and a place to live.

Even if what he wanted, now more than ever, was a friend.

"Justin?"

He spun around to face the one person who he hadn't considered would be here—Max Tremblay: Grady's boyfriend and the man whose life Justin had made miserable for several weeks a little over a year ago. With his heart pounding, Justin straightened and approached Max. "Ah, yes. Hello."

"What are you doing here?" Max was wearing a short-sleeve, collared shirt that showed off his defined forearms and biceps. Justin did his best to keep his gaze off the muscles and on Max's disapproving gaze. It wouldn't help his cause to be ogling Grady's partner.

"I found myself in the city and thought I might pay Grady a visit." Not really the truth, but not exactly a lie. The middle ground he always loved to walk.

Max closed the distance between them. "You don't find yourself anywhere you don't want to be." He crossed his arms and looked down at Justin. Having witnessed Max knock one of Grady's relatives out with a single punch, Justin was more than aware of the strength Max possessed. And Justin knew Max's strength went far beyond the physical; he'd been an emotional rock for Grady last year. Justin could only assume Max was still that for Justin's former ward.

"Not true. I once ended up in a bowling alley in Saskatoon. I can tell you that was absolutely accidental."

Max growled. "Why are you here? The truth without the bullshit."

Justin wasn't normally easily intimidated. He'd learned how to protect himself early on in his life, using his wit and his words more than his physical prowess. It was far easier to cut people down with a sharp tongue than a fist.

But Max was Grady's boyfriend, and given everything that had transpired between them last year, Justin couldn't help but feel a certain degree of trepidation about him. "I've left Vancouver, and I'm looking for work here."

Max's gaze narrowed. "Grady's dad didn't put you up to this? I know things are a bit better between them, but if he thinks he can get involved, start controlling him again—"

"No. I haven't spoken to Theo since I quit." When Max frowned, and cocked his head, Justin smiled. "Grady didn't tell you that?"

"He didn't."

"Before the wedding, I told Grady what I thought he needed to hear, and then I quit. I was pleased when I'd learned that he'd moved here to be with you. It's good to know that he's finally happy."

No longer being a key part of Grady's life might have broken Justin's heart, but he cared for Grady. If he wasn't the one who'd be able to make Grady smile, then Justin was happy that person turned out to be Max.

Max glanced around, his hands on his hips and a frown on his face. "If you're looking for work, why are you here? No offense, but you're not exactly personal trainer material."

Justin sniffed, lifting his chin. "I've done my fair share of working out. Just because I'm not built like yourself, doesn't mean that I'm not fit."

Max's annoyed expression morphed into a grin. "That's not what I said. Though it's good to know I can ruffle your feathers if I need to."

Justin forced his body to relax. He'd thought he'd gotten past his annoyance at Max's ability to tell-it-like-it-is, but apparently not. "Me coming here was a terrible idea. I'm going to head back to the hotel. Tell Grady I said hello." He spun around and marched down the sidewalk toward where he hoped he'd find a taxi.

"Justin, wait." Max caught up to him and placed a hand on his shoulder, stopping him dead in his tracks. "I'm sorry. Can we start over?"

"I don't think that's a good idea. It was a mistake, me coming here." Justin pushed the bridge of his glasses up his nose once more, annoyed by their pressure.

Max motioned at Justin's face. "Those are new."

"I needed a new prescription and my disposable contacts were no longer fiscally viable." One more annoying reminder of the life he'd left behind.

"They suit you." Max smiled. "Come back to the gym."

The warmth in Max's voice eased the tension in Justin's back. "I don't want to start something."

"I can see that." Max let his hand fall to his side. "Look, I know Grady will want to say hi to you. I was here to take him out to lunch, but the two of you should go instead."

Damn it, why did he have to be so fucking gallant? "I wouldn't want to disrupt your date."

Max rolled his eyes. "Just come to the gym. Talk to Grady like you'd been planning to and we'll go from there. Okay?"

The familiar urge to lash out, to keep the other person on edge so Justin could get what he wanted flashed in him. He closed his eyes and took a breath before nodding. "Thank you."

Max thankfully said nothing else as they retraced their steps to the gym. Justin couldn't help but mentally evaluate everything about Ringside the closer they got. There'd been a number of changes since the last time he'd been in Toronto. The sandwich board sign, which currently announced a weekend-warrior training class, hadn't been there. Neither had the obviously brand-new, yet retro sign over the front door. The latter was the perfect blend of old and new, nostalgia and leading edge.

"The front isn't what I expected." Justin slowed his pace, making sure to look around at the surrounding businesses. "It certainly stands out."

Max smiled as he put his hands on his hips. "Zack and Nolan did a great job bringing everything up to snuff. Russel, the previous owner, would have loved it."

A glance through the window told Justin that it wasn't overly busy inside. "You don't have much of a lunch crowd."

"It's Tuesday. Most of the people are upstairs at the lunch yoga class." When Justin turned and frowned at Max, the man simply shrugged. "Nolan's idea. It's turned out to be pretty popular."

"Interesting." Justin adjusted the strap of his duffel bag, doing his best to ignore the ache in his shoulder.

Max must have noticed, because in the next moment he was holding the gym door open for him. "Grady's inside. Come on."

Justin's chest tightened, making him painfully aware of each breath he pulled in. It would be easy to walk away from this, to find a library with a computer and make another list of jobs that he'd qualify for. Despite his reputation, he'd be able to find something. *Right?*

He stepped inside.

The gym smelled of sweat and cleaning supplies. There was a huge boxing ring in the middle of the room, a relic from a bygone age when men had felt the need to beat each other senseless to prove their worth. As he watched two women circling one another, protective headgear covering their faces and boxing gloves making their arms look like match sticks, he realized that stupidity was no longer relegated to men.

"Sandra is going for the women's featherweight competition next month." Max pointed to the smaller of the two women. "She's brutal. I won't go near the ring with her in it."

"Charming." Justin had never been a person for physical violence. He'd never once found it necessary.

Max led him toward a small office, that currently appeared empty. "Why don't you wait in there and I'll find Grady. I'm sure he's out back somewhere."

Justin nodded and dropped his duffel bag to the floor before taking a seat in the guest chair. The walls of the office were covered with picture frames. Each one held a photo that depicted life at Ringside Gym. Some were clearly old, the colors faded and the paper creased. Some were new and showed smiling faces of old and young people, all dressed to box.

One picture directly behind the desk, front and center on the wall, was a framed photo of three men. Max was easy to pick out. Presumably, the other two men were Zack and Eli, Max's friends. The three were all involved with the gym in some manner or other, having attended the facility as teens.

Justin had never had that experience, that form of camaraderie as a youth. He was an only child, and his parents had been far too busy to take him to activities growing up. He'd had his books, his computer, and the library, even if he'd lacked friends to share his ideas with. He'd taken classes, learned whatever he could about any topic of interest on his own. Words had become his companions, and it hadn't taken him long to master their use.

A chorus of loud voices behind him caught Justin's attention. Turning in his seat, he saw one of the men from the picture walking toward the boxing ring. Sporting a shaved head and a short beard, he appeared every inch a fighter. Justin couldn't take his eyes off him, which was why he jumped at the sound of Grady clearing his throat.

"That's Eli. He's pretty impressive to look at."

Justin smiled at Grady's sudden appearance. His heart pounded and his mouth went dry as he gave his head a shake. "Hello."

Grady was as handsome as ever. His skin was tanned and there was a sparkle in his brown eyes. His black curly hair was fashionably slicked back, the curled ends kissing his cheek. He appeared far more relaxed than the last time Justin had seen him. Obviously, life in Toronto had been good to him.

Grady smirked. "I didn't believe Max when he said you were here."

God, he's so happy. Justin let his gaze linger a tad longer than he should, but in that moment he realized he was okay with the idea that Grady had found happiness with someone else. His feelings, while still full of love for the boy who'd grown to become the man standing in front of him, weren't romantically driven. And that was as much of a shock to him as it probably would be to Grady.

His shoulders relaxed. "I found myself in town and was curious as to how you were doing. I thought I'd stop by and say hello."

"Justin, we've known each other far too long for bullshit." Grady came into the office and closed the door. "Why don't you tell me what's going on? Is this about Father?"

The verbal jab hurt more than Justin would have guessed. "Not at all. I haven't spoken to him since I quit." The mere thought of Theo Barnes made Justin's stomach turn. Justin had done far too many things for that man, most of which had put him at odds with Grady.

"Then what?" As Grady sat on the edge of the desk, Justin couldn't help but feel that for the first time in their acquaintance, Justin was at a disadvantage. "Everything you do and say has a purpose, and Toronto isn't exactly next door to Vancouver."

It was Justin's turn to look away. The unexpected concern in Grady's gaze was too much for him to deal with at the moment. Especially if he wanted a chance to make things right. Taking a slow, deep breath, Justin relaxed as much as he was able. "I need your help."

"Okay." Grady gave Justin's arm a squeeze. "What's the problem and what can I do?"

"It's as simple as that? All I have to do is ask and you'll drop everything and come to my rescue?" Given all of the crap that Justin had put Grady through when he was younger—their relationship had been rocky at best—he'd expected to do some groveling to get to this point.

Grady pinched the bridge of his nose before letting out a throaty chuckle. "We never seem to be able to talk like normal people." His hand fell to his lap, and he smiled. "Maybe we need to start over. Hi, Justin. I'm really happy to see you. How have you been? I was worried about you when you fell off the map before Lincoln's wedding. No one knew where you'd gone."

Justin's throat tightened. The sincerity in Grady's voice was overwhelming. "I'm . . . okay. I needed some time to myself, to think. You and Lincoln appeared to have your lives under control, and I knew the last thing you needed was me butting in places I wasn't wanted. Distance seemed like the best option."

"You know, I actually missed having you around." Grady shrugged when Justin snorted. "What? I did. You've been a part of my life for ten years. I felt like I'd lost a weirdly shaped extra limb."

"I have no doubt Max was more than happy to help fill the gap."

"Good to see you haven't lost your sense of snark. And I'm serious. I missed you."

Unshed tears squeezed his throat and made it difficult for him to swallow, forcing him to clear it once again. "I missed you as well."

Grady turned away. "If you show the least bit of emotion here, I'm going to cry, and that won't end well for either of us."

He was right, and Justin knew they'd both dissolve into a blubbering mess if given half a chance. Instead he straightened up and smiled. "Fine. Do you know what I don't miss? Not having to clean up your messes. God, you were a pain in the ass."

"Not something you have to worry about any longer. I'm like a real adult now and everything." Grady chuckled as he got up from the desk and sat in the chair beside Justin. "Okay, we've mastered the small-talk section of our day. Now, what can I help you with?"

Taking a beat to get his thoughts together, Justin turned to look squarely at Grady. Best to rip the bandage off. "I need help finding a job. I can't live in Vancouver any longer. I'd burned too many professional bridges over the years working for your father to find a position where my talents will be wanted there. Toronto seemed the next logical place."

"Oh, how the mighty have fallen." Grady laughed.

Justin recoiled as that stab cut him deep. "If it's going to be a problem, I'll leave." He started to stand, wanting to put some distance between them.

"No, no." Grady put his hand on Justin's arm and encouraged him to sit back down. "I'm sorry. Old habits."

Justin nodded. "Fine."

"Have you spoken with your parents?"

Justin rolled his eyes on reflex. "Of course. My lack of employment is the primary topic of conversation with every phone call."

"They won't help you?"

Grady didn't know everything regarding Justin's relationship with his parents, so Justin forgave him for asking. "They don't exactly have the sort of connections that would be useful." Not to mention that his mom had flat out refused to let him move home again.

"And you think I'll be able to help?" Grady sat back, his frown making him look years older. "I don't have many connections here personally, but I can see what Zack and Max might be able to come up with. They're both well-known in the business community and can send out feelers."

Even having that small measure of a plan helped Justin relax. "I would appreciate that. And I won't be waiting around. I'll be talking to some headhunters to see what options are out there for me."

Grady nodded. "What about a place to live? Where are you staying?"

"I'm in a hotel for the moment. I only arrived this morning. I'll need to be out by the end of the week. I . . . don't have much in the way of accessible cash right now. I've pretty much burned up everything that I had in my savings."

Grady got to his feet so fast, Justin's breath caught. "Hang on. I have an idea."

"Wait, where are you going?"

"Just hold on. Stay there." He was out the office door before Justin had time to speak.

Typical Grady. Justin also rose, his back already aching from the thin padding on the seat and the awkward angle, and he stepped out into the main gym. This was such a strange place to find himself, the polar opposite to the libraries and bookstores he'd loved growing up. Sure, he'd spent his fair share of time in gyms over the years, mostly taking spin and kettlebell classes. They helped to relieve stress. But a boxing gym? Never in his wildest imagination had he thought he'd ever set foot in a place like this.

A man walked through the front door, catching Justin's attention. His blond hair spilled out the sides of a Blue Jays ball hat and his jogging pants were riding low on his hips. The man winked at Justin as he passed on his way to the changing room. It had been a long time since a man had turned his head. He'd grown so used to putting his personal needs second that he didn't know how to process flirting.

Not that he was about to chase the man into the dressing room and ask for his number. That wasn't Justin's style.

The handsome newcomer had apparently caught the attention of another gym member as well; the man was tall, with short-cut black hair and the most amazing crystal-blue eyes Justin had ever seen. His gaze met Justin's briefly, sending a full-body tingle rolling through him. The blue-eyed man blushed before he squared his shoulders and went back to hitting the heavy bag hanging from the beam.

"Justin!" Justin turned at the sound of Grady's voice, surprised when he was flanked by Max and the third man from the picture. "This is Zack Anderson, owner of Ringside. Zack, this is Justin, an old family friend."

Justin shook Zack's hand, and couldn't help but assess his character through the strength of his grip. "Nice to meet you."

Zack was taller than him by a few inches, and his aura screamed businessman. "Grady here says that you need a job and a place to stay."

"Yes. He mentioned that you might have some contacts who you could put me in touch with." This wasn't a handout, simply a friend doing him a favor. No reason whatsoever to feel like a failure for accepting what was being offered.

"I do. I also have a proposition for you." Zack crossed his arms and looked at Justin in a way that made Justin sure he wouldn't like what was coming.

"What's that?"

"How would you like to live and work at the gym until you find an alternative?"

Justin cocked an eyebrow. "Do I get to sleep in the ring? Or is there a cot in the locker room?"

Grady chuckled. "I told you he was a smart-ass."

"You did, and Justin, no, you don't have to worry about staying in here." Zack indicated for him to follow, and they moved farther into the building. "I own the whole building, and we've been working on getting the rest of it renovated now that the gym is mostly finished. There are a few apartments that I want to convert, maybe make them executive suites. Exactly the sort of thing that I could use someone to help me develop and promote." Zack led him to an internal stairwell and up to the third floor.

"Given all the work you did with Father, I figured you would have tons of insights." Grady's voice echoed in the stairwell. "What do you think?"

The hallway they stepped into was clean enough, though it was clear no one had lived up here in quite some time. Justin waited for Zack to unlock the door closest to them, before following behind him. The apartment walls were exposed brick, with large industrial-style windows lining one side. It was an open space, with a small, dated kitchen off to the left side.

There were also moldy cupboard doors, along with hardwood floors that had seen better days and the most unusual smell Justin had ever experienced in his life.

Zack moved through the empty space, growing more animated the longer he spoke. "It's not much now, but I have great plans for it. We've budgeted enough to convert one apartment immediately, which we'd use as a model to show potential clients. If you're interested, you can live here and help me with the development of the rental units until you find a better job."

Grady came up beside Justin and smiled. "He'd been talking about wanting to do this for a while now, but hadn't reached out to anyone who had the experience. It's a win-win for both of you."

Crossing the room to where Zack stood, Justin laced his hands behind his back. "Free rent and a small stipend while the renovations are underway. I won't be able to look for other employment while I'm working on this, and I do occasionally like to eat. I'll also need a budget and timeline to see if what you're proposing is feasible—I'm done trying to work miracles in my professional life. Grady burned that out of me. And the windows need to be opened up. I'm not sure I want to know what that smell is."

Zack grinned. "You and I are going to get along just fine." He stuck out his hand. "I'll do up a contract. You have a deal."

Justin shook on it and, for the first time since he left Vancouver, felt the pieces of his life slipping back into place.

═ CHAPTER ═
TWO

Finn's arms and legs were shaking long after he'd finished his workout. He'd pushed himself harder than he'd ever done before, mostly because of his mortification at being caught staring at Leo by the newcomer to the gym. It didn't matter that the man hadn't a clue who Finn was, or the sad state of his total infatuation with Leo. It was the fact that another human had witnessed Finn's slip that had mortified him.

Jesus, he was acting like a hormone-riddled teen.

His knuckles and wrists were sore from the pounding he'd given the heavy bag. Eli had been pushing him pretty hard in recent weeks. He hadn't realized how hard it would be having him as his personal trainer, but he should have realized that a former MMA fighter wouldn't take things easy on anyone. As he unwound the wrap from his hands, Finn did his best to ignore the throbbing. He needed a shower, and then he'd be able to head home. King would be antsy for his walk, and Finn had some work to do afterward. The exact same things he tended to do every night.

"I swear, the little fucker sucker punched me."

Finn froze at the sound of Leo's voice echoing from the hallway. It was low, gravelly, as though he smoked a pack of cigarettes a day. There was something primal about it that sent shivers through Finn. Leo came into the dressing room with his two friends, Ron and Lucas. Yup, he'd been stalking Leo long enough to learn who his friends were, where he worked, and that he absolutely hated losing in the ring.

Ron chuckled. "Dude, Eli doesn't need to land a cheap shot to win. You just suck compared to him."

Finn realized he was staring at the trio, and jerked his attention back to the task of removing his wraps.

"I know." Leo groaned as he plopped onto the bench. "Someday I'm going to win."

Lucas snorted. "Keep telling yourself that."

As much as Finn might have a crush on Leo, he had to agree. Eli was a monster in the ring, and no one at Ringside was trained enough to come close to beating him in a match.

Leo leaned over and tapped the bench where Finn sat. "Hey, you work with Eli. What are his weaknesses?"

It took a count of three before Finn's brain recognized the fact that Leo—beautiful, strong Leo—was actually speaking to him. Finn opened his mouth, but nothing came out.

Lucas nodded. "See, even he can't think of anything. You're screwed, dude."

The trio finished getting changed and disappeared into the shower area, leaving Finn sitting there feeling the fool. Why was he like this? If he was on the phone for work, he could talk someone's ear off. He could troubleshoot and walk them through the decision tree without a hiccup. It was a process, a straight line of logic that he could fall back on.

But in person, the pressure of having people there listening, their expectations clear for him to see, it became too much.

And God help him if the other person was someone he was attracted to. His brain would freeze, and he wouldn't be able to get a single sentence out.

He'd come out a lot later in life than most gay men, but it wasn't as though he'd never dated. Well, he hadn't dated a lot. And the last man he'd had any interest in had been Eli's husband Devan, three years ago.

Still, this shouldn't be that hard. He knew Leo was gay and currently single. All Finn had to do was talk to him, to stand up and introduce himself: *Hi, I'm Finn and I've been sort of stalking you for three months now. Wanna go out?* What could possibly go wrong? Worst case, Leo would say he wasn't interested, and that would be it. That was all it would be: romantic rejection. Just because every man he'd gone out with—all three of them—had brushed him aside after one or two dates, didn't mean there was anything wrong with him. Maybe he sucked at putting himself out there.

Or he didn't inspire romantic love.

Yeah, no problem at all.

He couldn't use the showers now that Leo and his friends were in there. Finn's cock would get hard, and that would make for an awkward conversation.

Instead, he grabbed his clothing, threw it into his gym bag, and headed out. He'd barely made it into the main gym area, when Eli jogged over. "There you are. I missed seeing your last set. How did you make out?"

Finn really liked Eli as a friend, but he was so fit, so handsome, that Finn had a hard time looking him in the eyes. "Good. My hands and wrists are a bit sore from the impact."

"I'll have to check your stance next time. I don't want you getting hurt." Eli put his hands on his hips. "Devan wanted me to check in with you to see how you're doing. He said you canceled your coffee date with him last week."

Finn had met Eli's husband when he'd had to do an upgrade to the Canadian Blood Services computer system in Toronto. Devan was so easygoing that Finn had found himself connecting with him in a way he didn't normally do with others. Thankfully, Devan had been aware of Finn's feelings, without Finn letting on, and had informed him that he wasn't looking for a relationship. Having Devan as a friend ended up being way better for Finn in the long run. Even if he felt awkward around the happy couple.

He didn't have the heart to tell Devan that he was overwhelmed by how happy his friend currently was. It sounded petty, made Finn feel like an asshole, and was plain wrong. "I wasn't feeling great and didn't want him to catch anything."

Eli waved that away. "Matthew brings home every bug from the daycare. Devan wanted to know if you were going to the speed dating event?"

God, the speed dating fund-raiser that Ringside Gym was putting on had been the talk of the facility since Nolan had come up with the idea. "I don't think so."

"That's what I figured you'd say." Eli cocked his head "You probably know what he'd say too."

Finn smiled. "That I'll never find someone if I don't keep putting myself out there."

"He's right. And if nothing else, you'd be supporting a good cause."

"You're going after my soft spots, aren't you?"

"I don't take prisoners." Eli's smirk would have made the devil blush. "I'll make sure Nolan marks you as attending."

"I didn't say that I'd go."

"But you will." Eli gave Finn's arm a pat. "Don't try and hide from Devan. He'll track you down if he thinks you're avoiding him."

"I'm not. I won't." Finn groaned. "I'll see him for coffee next week. Promise."

Before Finn turned to leave, he noticed the newcomer who'd caught him staring at Leo earlier coming out from the back office. With his glasses and perfectly trimmed haircut, the man would have fit in at a bank, rather than at the gym. "Who's that?"

Eli glanced back over his shoulder. "Not sure. I see he's with Grady though. Maybe a friend?"

"Maybe. He sure doesn't look like a new member."

"You didn't either your first few visits."

"It didn't take long for you to whip me into shape." Finn's muscles hadn't stopped aching since their first session. "Maybe you'll get yourself another client?"

"Possibly." Before Finn could move, Eli turned. "Grady!"

Shit. "I should get going." Finn had only managed to take a step away when Grady came over. He couldn't walk away now without coming across as an asshole. *God, today could just end now. Please. Thank you.* Clutching the strap of his gym bag with both hands, Finn wanted to fade into the background.

Grady gave them a wide grin. "Eli, this is my friend Justin McCormick. He's new to town and has agreed to help Zack with the apartment development project." Grady moved to the side to let Justin join the group. "Justin, this is Eli."

Justin gave off an annoyed vibe. His brown eyes appeared sharp, assessing everyone in a nanosecond. The glasses were a sexy touch, though. "Nice to meet you. I'm sorry your last fight appearance didn't end well for you."

"I'm not." Eli straightened to his full height. "So, you've agreed to work with Zack, eh?"

If Justin was intimidated by Eli's posturing, he didn't let it show. "Yes. Grady seems to think my expertise will be beneficial to the project."

"As long as we get rid of the stick up your ass, I think you'll do just fine." Grady's gaze locked on to Finn. "Well, hello, handsome." He stuck out his hand. "Grady Barnes. I've seen you around here."

"Finn Miller." Finn shook Grady's hand, realizing a moment too late that his palm was sweaty. *Wonderful.*

"He's a friend of Devan's and one of my clients." Eli kept his gaze on Justin as he spoke. "Are you attending the speed dating fundraiser?"

Justin raised an eyebrow. "Wasn't even aware of it."

Grady chuckled. "You're going."

"While I appreciate your help finding a job and a place to stay, I'm more than capable of finding my own dates." There was something about the way Justin shoved his hands into his pockets that made him seem like a nervous teenager. Or maybe like Finn, he wasn't too keen on the idea of being thrust into a social situation where he'd have to play pretend. Finn understood that.

"It's a fund-raiser to help get our LGBTQ after-school self-defense class going." Grady narrowed his gaze at Finn. "You're going, right?" Before Finn could respond, Grady had turned back to Justin. "See, you'll know at least one other person there. You have to go."

Justin's gaze locked on to Finn's, and for a moment Finn could have sworn Justin was able to read his thoughts. The blush that immediately heated his face wasn't surprising, but annoyed the hell out of him. Needing to get out of here before his embarrassment became too much, Finn smiled. "It was nice meeting you all. Eli, let Devan know that I'll see him next week."

A quick turn and then he made a beeline for the door. It was only after the wind hit his sweat-damp body that Finn realized he must have looked like hell. Of course, he had to be sweaty and disgusting when being introduced to two handsome men at once. That was how his life went. Which was the main reason he couldn't go to the speed dating night. He'd spend all his time getting ready, and no doubt he'd land flat on his face—either verbally flailing, or doing something else to make himself appear a fool. His nerves would get the better of him, and he'd spend the entire thirty seconds of each date trying to sputter out a hello.

No, best to make a small donation to the cause and stay home.

Justin watched Finn leave the gym, his face turning a shade of red Justin had never seen on a person before. "You really are clueless sometimes, Grady."

"What's that supposed to mean?" It was funny to see Grady's wide-eyed innocence once again, even if Justin no longer believed it.

"It means that you embarrassed that man. He has no intention of coming to your stupid event, and he didn't appreciate being cornered."

Grady rolled his eyes. "I didn't embarrass him. And he'll enjoy it. All he needs is a little convincing. Isn't that right. Eli?"

Eli was obviously not going to get involved with this conversation. "Finn is a good guy and a better friend. Just make sure you behave around him." Without another word, Eli turned and walked back to the ring in the center of the gym.

Justin couldn't help but watch Eli walk away. He cocked his eyebrow as he turned toward Grady. "I see there is more than one person to keep you in line."

Grady chuckled. "Yeah, you could say that."

"You really don't need me anymore."

Grady shrugged. "I haven't for a while."

Tension that Justin hadn't realized he'd been holding in his shoulders bled away. "I'm glad."

Grady gave him another small smile, before he started toward the main doors of the gym. "Where are your things right now?"

"Back at the hotel."

"Why don't you go get them, and then I can take you out for supper and you can stay with us tonight. We can talk about next steps and I can make sure that you have what you need to get going for the project." Grady hesitated, before smiling. "I'll make Max take us to a nice place for supper."

Justin could only imagine what that would mean. "I'm at your mercy."

And that was a new experience all unto itself.

══ CHAPTER ══ THREE

J ustin should've realized that supper wasn't going to go as planned the moment he climbed into the back seat of Max's car. There was a look in his eyes that screamed, *Payback time.* "I know Grady promised you a fancy dinner, but I have some obligations I couldn't get out of. I promise you, the food where we're going is great."

Grady slid into the front seat and kissed Max for so long that Justin had to look away. When they separated, Grady patted Max's cheek. "So, you're changing our plans?"

"I have to. Sorry." Max didn't sound the least bit apologetic.

"It's fine. But I'm totally going to make you pay for it later."

Justin had never been so thankful to sit in the back seat of a vehicle before in his life. "Have I mentioned how disgustingly cute the two of you are? Please stop."

Max smiled at him in the rearview mirror. "Yes, sir."

The drive through Toronto traffic gave him time to relax. In a matter of hours he'd found, at least temporarily, a job and a place to stay. He had companionship for the evening, even if it was going to be more than a little awkward.

The constant squeeze that had gripped his chest for months now, eased. He could breathe without uncertainty, without doubt clawing at the back of his brain, making him question every move he'd made in the past year. The last two months in particular had been too much for him. His mother had made it clear that while she felt sorry for his situation, it was one of his own making. *"You've stayed with us for six months now. I raised you better than to leave a position without having something else lined up. Consider this a lesson for you. One I shouldn't have to teach you at your age."*

Justin knew better than to reach out to his parents again, especially after the last conversation he'd had with his mom. She'd been right that he shouldn't have quit without having something else lined up. It had gone against not only his better judgment, but everything he'd been taught.

His parents weren't horrible people. They always meant well, but their interest in having a child had had more to do with their public persona and less with the urge to love and care for another being. His own relationship with his parents had been the template he'd used when helping to raise Grady. Which no doubt had been the crux of most of their problems over the years.

Max pulled the car around the back of Frantic, Max's nightclub. Justin sat up, interested again. He'd only seen the alley behind the bar on the night he'd tried to bribe Max to stay away from Grady. His previous time in Toronto hadn't allowed for him to socialize, not when he'd been tasked with dragging Grady back to Vancouver for his brother's wedding.

It made sense that if Max had an engagement he couldn't break, it would take place at his bar. "What time do you open?"

"We have two hours before the crowds show up. I need to meet with the DJ before then for our monthly system check." Max pulled into a reserved parking spot. "Grady said you like cheeseburgers. I called ahead and had the kitchen make some for us."

Grady turned around to face Justin. "I promise, it'll be the best you'll ever have."

Justin followed the two of them into the bar, trying his best to keep his gaze averted when Grady leaned against Max and touched a random spot on his body. Every contact between them felt like a small knife turning in his side. It didn't hurt the way it once had, but neither was it an experience he wanted to prolong. Perhaps coming to Toronto hadn't been his best idea.

"I can get you anything you'd like to drink." Max was moving around behind the bar like an expert. The DJ was setting up for the evening, loud music echoing in the mostly empty room. "Are you a Scotch drinker? Or do you prefer something a little lighter?"

Justin didn't know what he was these days. "Whatever you have is fine with me."

Grady was staring at him, disbelief on his face. "That's not the Justin I remember."

"What's that supposed to mean?" But then Grady was probably the only person in the world who honestly knew Justin. It wasn't a surprise that he'd call Justin on his abnormal behavior.

"It means that you are a huge Scotch snob, and I very much doubt that Max has anything back there that would meet your high standards."

"Hey!" Max stopped moving behind the bar, his hands on his hips. "I'll have you know I've improved my stock since our trip to Vancouver."

Grady chuckled. "Sure you have."

Max turned to Justin, his gaze narrowed. "Are you certain you weren't sent here to take him back home? I'd be more than happy to buy a ticket for you."

Despite his mood, Justin couldn't help but smile. "No, he's all yours."

Max groaned as he grabbed a bottle of Scotch from the top shelf. "I don't know if I should give you this, then. I was hoping someone might take him off my hands."

The amber of the Macallan filled Justin's class, swirling around the near-perfect glass. It had been quite a while since he had indulged, having finished his last bottle of Scotch over a month ago. It hadn't seemed right to partake in such a luxury when he was budgeting every last dime. *Oh, how the mighty have fallen.* He took a sip and sighed. "Bless you."

Max winked at him. "You're welcome."

"Don't I get anything?" Grady batted his eyelashes at Max until he poured him a Coke. "Thank you, handsome."

Justin hadn't been certain that the two of them were going to make it as a couple when he had last seen them. Grady being Grady, there had always been a chance that the idiot would have been too stubborn to see what had been right in front of him. But as painful as it might be to no longer have Grady's undivided attention, it gave Justin hope to see that he'd managed to move past the pain of his mother's death and father's controlling nature, to have a healthy relationship with Max.

It was time for Justin to move forward and start building some healthy relationships of his own. That was what this trip to Toronto was all about. A chance to start over, a chance to become his own man and not be beholden to someone, such as Grady's father. Years ago, he had jumped from his own family and the controlling nature of his mother, right into the viper's nest that was the Barnes household, when he'd barely had time to figure out whom he was and what he wanted. Then his priorities had had to be pushed aside so he could practically raise Grady. He was free of all of that now, and he had to take steps forward and get on with his life.

Three plates of cheeseburgers and fries were placed in front of them on the bar. The bouncer was doubling as a waiter, and not a very good one at that, as he dropped the plates of food in front of them. Justin gave him the side-eye as the brute of a man ambled away. "I've been promised that this is a good meal."

"Don't be such a snob." Grady picked up his burger, took a huge bite, getting a drop of ketchup on the side of his mouth.

In a blink, Max reached out and swiped the errant drop from his boyfriend's lips. "I can't take you anywhere."

"I know of a few places you can take me." Grady winked at him, and there was no mistaking the lust in his tone.

Justin shook his head. "Dear God, the two of you are even more disgusting now than you were the last time I saw you."

"We really are." Max licked the ketchup from his thumb.

Justin fought back an eye roll as he took a bite of his burger. "Mmm. That's excellent."

"I'll pass on your compliments to the chef." Max nodded. "So, what are your plans for the next little while?"

"I plan to begin work on Zach's project tomorrow."

"That's good. Then you'll have some money to buy some new clothing so you'll be all ready for the speed dating event." Grady smiled, clearly knowing full well that mentioning the event would get under Justin's skin. The downside to having your young ward now grown and more annoying than ever.

"I have no intention of attending . . . whatever the hell that event is."

"Speed dating." Max shoved a few French fries into his mouth. "You must have at least heard of it?"

"I'm not an idiot, nor have been living in the dark ages. But I don't need to be shoved in front of potential mates for an awkward eight minutes of conversation."

"It's more like three minutes." Grady shrugged, a smirk firmly fixed on his face. "Even you can be charming for three minutes in a row."

Max snorted.

Grady straightened. "What, you don't think my boy can win the heart of a suitor?"

"In three minutes?" Max looked at Justin and shrugged. "Nope."

"You're wrong. Justin can totally get a date in three minutes."

Max stood up straighter. "That sounds like a bet. Are you making a bet, little man?"

Grady's smirk blossomed into a full-blown grin. "I am absolutely making that a bet. What's the wager going to be for?"

Justin silently groaned. "I am not being a part of any wager. Nor am I going to this—"

"You have no say at all." Grady leaned further onto the bar. "The winner gets to pick any restaurant in Toronto to eat at."

Max crossed his arms. "Okay. And? Because there's no way you'll leave it at that."

Grady's grin turned positively Satanic. "And the loser has to wear that thing I bought last month. For a week."

"Fuck that." Max uncrossed his arms. "One day."

"Three days." Grady clicked his tongue. "With the possibility of a reduced sentence for good behavior."

Justin had no idea what this *thing* was, and had a sneaking suspicion he didn't want to know. Best to let the two of them affectionately torture one another in private.

Max seemed to consider the idea for a moment before he nodded. "Fair enough. What are the rules and the condition for winning?"

"Justin has to attend the speed dating event, he has to talk to more than five people, and he has to receive more than three requests for a date." Grady picked up his French fry and sucked on it. "What do you think?"

"I think that is a pretty tall order, especially for Justin."

Justin waved his hands. "I *am* sitting right here."

Both men shushed him, and for the first time in his life, Justin appreciated how he'd made Grady feel for all those years.

Max shook his head. "Are you sure you want to go with that? I mean more than three requests for a date? Why don't we say at least one request, that way you'll have a fighting chance?"

"Deal." Grady stood up and stuck out his hand. "I have faith in him."

Justin wasn't certain that he had the same confidence in himself. "The two of you are ridiculous." He should hop on the next flight to Vancouver while his sanity was still intact.

"Are you just figuring that out now?" Max smiled and then went back to eating his cheeseburger. "I'm liking my chances of winning this bet."

"No way. My boy Justin here is going to prove you wrong." Grady faced Justin. "And you are not going to let me down on this one. You owe me."

"While that may be, and to reiterate, I have no intention of attending this event. I have more important things to figure out before I am remotely ready to consider dating."

Chancing a glance over at Grady, Justin didn't like the excitement that was shining in his eyes. When Grady got one of his crazy ideas, there was very little that anybody could do to stop him. Having seen the end results of Grady's attentions before, Justin could only brace himself for the inevitable.

He really didn't want to be on the receiving end of Grady's enthusiasm. He especially didn't want Grady meddling in his personal affairs. *Payback's a bitch.*

"Dude, this is a fund-raiser to help troubled teens. LGBTQ teens, kids who need to figure their shit out. A whole bunch of kids just like I was." Grady leaned his elbow on the bar, bracing his head on his hand. "While you might be a prick, I know you're not so much of an asshole as to walk away from an opportunity to help the less fortunate. Come on, man, think of the kids."

Of course, Grady knew all of Justin's weak spots. "I can't afford to buy my own alcohol, let alone make a donation."

"But you are going to, right?"

"Unlikely." Another lie, and from the look on Grady's face, he knew it as well. "However, if I find some extra funds between now and then, I might *consider* attending. When is this stupid thing?"

Max groaned. "Please tell me that it wasn't that easy. Justin, where's that badass, take-no-shit personality of yours that I'd grown to loath?"

"Apparently, I left it in Vancouver." Plus, it was fun to watch Max squirm.

"The speed dating event is in five days." Grady laughed. "And yes, it was absolutely that easy. I told you I knew my boy. He might have all these—" Grady waved his hands in the space between them "—prickles around him, but I know he has a gooey center in there somewhere."

"I would never have guessed." Max shook his head. "You have my condolences, Justin."

"Thanks." Once again, Justin was equal parts annoyed and impressed how Grady had talked him into doing something that he didn't want to do. "Though, I think he'll have a harder time with the next two steps."

"That's what I'm hoping for." Max's eyes widened. "No offense."

"It would take more than that to offend me." He had accepted that truth about himself many years ago. Affection wasn't something that came easily to him, nor was it something that he had been encouraged to seek out. His parents had enjoyed his academic accomplishments, had been pleased at the numerous awards he had won as an orator as a teen. But they'd been strict and stingy when it came to doling out hugs.

It had taken him a long time to get used to Grady and his naturally affectionate touches when he had arrived at the Barnes household. Now as a thirty-seven-year-old, Justin had finally stopped flinching whenever someone touched him in kindness.

"I think we have freaked poor Justin out enough for one evening." Max refilled Justin's half-empty glass. "Tell me where you were thinking about starting on Zack's crazy project?"

Justin had hardly had time to consider his living arrangements, let alone know where he was going to start on the development project. "Tomorrow I'll take a look at the building, get a feel for what I have to work with. After that, I'll determine building permits and contracting options." It wasn't the most exciting project he had ever worked on, but it was something he was familiar with, something he could get his feet wet with, and use to establish his reputation in Toronto.

"I have no doubt you'll make the place amazing." Grady stole a French fry from Max's plate. "Who knows, maybe you'll turn it into a hot spot for bachelors and you won't want to leave."

Justin rolled his eyes. "For my horde of future dates? Maybe I'll set up a revolving door with single clients from the gym. I'll have to be sure to schedule them appropriately—I don't want the men to run into one another in the stairwell."

Max laughed. "You've changed, Justin. That's not a bad thing."

Had he? *I guess I have.* A lot had happened to him in the past six months, not all of it positive, but all of it had played a part in pulling him away from his old patterns of behavior and toward a different outlook on his life. Some of those transitions had been uncomfortable, and not exactly what he'd wanted, but he knew deep down that they had been the right things for him to do. Even if he had more he needed to accomplish.

Coming to Toronto was part of that fix, to address some of the mistakes he had made over the past few years. With any luck, this new project would set him on the right path to a happy life.

If that was something he was allowed to have.

CHAPTER FOUR

The ache in the back of Finn's neck was threatening to bleed into his head and cause a major headache. He'd spent the past three hours on the computer helping a client fix an issue with their server. While he enjoyed the fact that his position as a computer network specialist allowed him to work from home whenever he liked, he had a tendency to become engrossed in his task and not take breaks. Still, he'd always been awkward when forced into corporate social situations. Not because he didn't like people, but because his brain always came up with the ideal thing to say long after the conversation was over.

It was really annoying.

Working from home was far easier, not to mention he had an unending supply of coffee that kept him going long into the night. He set his own hours, worked when others were asleep, and was pretty much his own boss. The only downside was that he could go days on end without speaking to another person. If it wasn't for his workout sessions with Eli and the occasional coffee with Devan, Finn wouldn't hang out with friends at all.

King whined from where he sat beside Finn, looking up at him with those bulgy eyes that appeared far too big for his little pug face. Finn fished a dog bone from the bag on his computer desk and tossed it across the living room, sending his furry companion scurrying across the carpet.

Leaning back in his chair, his hands fell away from the keyboard. Despite what his parents thought, he didn't actually like his solitary life. His sessions at the gym, while sometimes awkward, were quickly becoming the highlight of his week. Partially, it had to do with Eli's understanding of his quiet nature. Their conversations were short, and Eli always gave him time to think. And when words were especially difficult, Eli encouraged him to vent his frustration on the heavy bag. Most of those times, Finn was thinking about Leo.

His computer beeped at him, indicating he had a new email. With a few quick clicks, he opened up the message.

Attention Ringside members:

This is a reminder of our first annual Fast Friends: Speed Dating for Youth event. Your fee of $50 will help fund the start-up of our LGTBQ self-defense course. Need more incentive? The first 20 members to arrive will receive a free Ringside Gym T-shirt!

Convinced? Sign up today by responding to this email.

We'll see you on Saturday.

Zack and Nolan

Crap. Finn really didn't want to go to that, and yet it was probably a good idea. The chance to get out and mingle with other people, to financially support an amazing resource for teens, and to potentially have the opportunity to speak with Leo was almost too good to pass up.

Unfortunately, if he actually got the chance to talk to Leo, the odds of him saying anything intelligent were low at best. It was more likely that he'd freeze completely, which would be a waste of everyone's time. It would be better for him to stay at home and watch Netflix than it would be for him to go and make an ass out of himself.

He deleted the email, and only felt a little bit guilty about it.

He managed to go an entire hour without thinking he was missing out. Then, his cell phone buzzed, and with a glance, he saw that it was Devan. *How long did it take you to delete the email?*

Finn smiled. *I gave it a full min. I'm not going.*

At least he hoped he wasn't going. Now that Devan was involved, it was quite likely things were about to change for him.

I know for a fact Leo will be there. I'm working on the attendance list . . .

Shit. This was the downside to his friend knowing his Achilles' heel. *I still don't want to go.*

But you will. I'm putting you down. I'll pay your fee.
Finn rolled his eyes. *You won't give up, will you?*
Nope. Eli says hi.
Tell Eli he's a traitor.
He says he's adding extra reps tomorrow.

Finn chuckled, though Eli probably wasn't kidding. *Tell him thanks.*

Tossing his phone onto the stack of papers beside his computer, Finn resigned himself to the fact that in four days, he was going to make a public embarrassment of himself. If nothing else, he'd show up, shake a few hands, and duck out before anyone knew he was gone. Devan wouldn't have wasted his money, Finn would be able to prove that he had been there, and maybe he would catch a glimpse of Leo. Though that would be it, because there was no way in hell he was going to be able to sit down at a table with Leo and string words together.

His inability to speak to people easily had been a pain point for him most of his life. He liked people, he liked being around people, but in the sense of being in the same room with them rather than conversing. One or two people on their own and he was fine. More than that and Finn would much rather sit back and listen. Words had never been his ally. Give him numbers or algorithms any day.

Speaking of which, he had at least another hour's worth of work to do before he could call it a day and take King out for his walk. He would have to worry about speed dating, friendships, and his obsessions at a later time. Rolling his head, he ignored the pain in his neck as best he could and continued problem solving.

Justin stood in the hallway that led to the third-floor apartments. The odor in the air was still there, so heavy with the scent of mold it had probably been absorbed into his clothing. When he had agreed to help Zach with this project, he should have negotiated danger pay. Or, at the least, an endless supply of facemasks. Dear God the *smell.*

At the first door, he had to fight to get the key into the lock. The metal scraped against the tumblers, as though it were trying to prevent Justin from gaining access. It couldn't be a good sign when the building itself was rejecting him.

Justin stepped inside and looked around for a place to set his duffel bag. Nothing had changed from what he had seen yesterday: the same exposed bricks, disintegrating kitchen cupboards, and pitted hardwood.

He'd had a brief meeting with Zach that morning. Now budgets, contractors, and an endless list of requirements spun around his brain. It was a lot to take on, but having an open-ended timeline for completion meant he would be able to do things right.

The first matter of business would be to clean up what was now his apartment so he wouldn't die in his sleep.

Grady had offered to help pay for some furniture, the very idea of which continued to make Justin cringe. He had promised himself that he wouldn't take another penny from any Barnes ever again, and though Grady's intentions were no doubt kind, Justin wasn't about to fall back into old habits. He could do this on his own. Even if that meant sleeping on an air mattress in a musty rundown apartment while he scoured ads on Kijiji for temporary items until he could buy new items to stage the place.

Finding a spot on the kitchen counter that didn't appear to have anything alive on it, Justin wandered around the room taking in as many details as he could. While the walls and cupboards were in bad shape, it wouldn't take much to make the place livable. It certainly wasn't his old penthouse, or the Barnes mansion in Vancouver, but he could make something of this.

"Hello."

Justin turned around and saw a thin man standing in the doorway, two buckets full of cleaning supplies in his hands.

"I'm Nolan, Zach's partner. He mentioned that you had come up here." Nolan looked around the apartment. "Whoa, Zach said things were rough, but I had no idea they were this bad. I haven't been in any of the apartments yet."

"And I foolishly agreed to live here." If it weren't for the fact that he needed the extra money he would save from not staying at the hotel for groceries, he would've waited to move in.

Nolan took a tentative step into the apartment. "I know the first time Zach brought me to the gym, I couldn't get over the decay of the place. It's hard to believe that the building was only empty for ten years." Nolan crossed the room and placed the two buckets on the counter beside Justin's duffel bag. "I thought you could use some help."

"I wouldn't want to take you away from your work downstairs."

"Not at all. You'll be doing me a favor letting me hide somewhere. More than a few people are annoyed at my enthusiasm for the speed dating event this Saturday."

"That was your brainchild? I seem to have been roped into attending myself."

"Grady?"

"I'm certain it's a punishment for all the years of torment he feels I gave him."

Nolan chuckled. "I promise it won't be as bad as you think. The Pear Tree will be catering, and I'll make sure you get one of the free T-shirts. You can use it to work around here. It will save some of your other clothing."

Justin was a good judge of character, a necessary skill in negotiation and business dealings. Nolan was clearly someone who genuinely liked people. Having him around would be a nice change of pace. "It would be great to have a hand, at least until I can get . . . whatever that smell is out of the air."

Nolan reached into one of the buckets and pulled out a large pair of pink rubber gloves. "I have two. We can do an assessment of the apartment as we go. I have some great contacts for contractors who helped with the gym downstairs. I don't think it will take too long to make this apartment perfect."

Without another word, Nolan removed the remaining supplies from the bucket and started working. Justin didn't have a lot of experience with manual labor; it hadn't exactly been encouraged in his household. But he knew his way around a scrub brush, if for no other reason than he absolutely hated a messy bathroom. Slipping a bright-pink rubber glove onto each hand, he grabbed one of the now-empty buckets and moved to the sink.

The pipes rattled the moment he turned the water on, but nothing immediately came out, other than a few spits of water. There was a loud bang as an explosion of brown liquid erupted from the spout, sending Justin jumping back.

"I had the plumbing fixed downstairs before anything was opened. I never realized how bad it was throughout the entire building." Nolan peeked over Justin's shoulder, groaning slightly at the mess in the sink. "I have my plumber on speed dial. Let me give him a call and see if he has time to stop by sometime this week."

"I guess that means I'll be without running water for a while."

"You're more than welcome to use the bathroom and showers downstairs. I'll have Zach order an extra watercooler so you have fresh water to drink until we get this sorted."

With the water looking a little less suspect, Justin slipped the bucket under the stream and added cleaning solution. "It'll be good enough for cleaning."

The two of them began the daunting task of scrubbing down the kitchen. Justin wasn't a social creature by nature, but he found it quite easy to slip into conversation with Nolan. It was hard to believe that this man suffered from crippling anxiety. That had been one of the things both Max and Grady had mentioned to him, stressing that if Justin did anything to upset Nolan, he'd have to face a very angry Zack.

"The majority of people are out of here by ten at night, and we don't open until ten in the morning. The bathrooms are all yours whenever you want, but that's when you'll have the most privacy." Nolan brushed his fringe from his face, and Justin caught sight of a long scar. He tried to look away, but his brain latched on to how Nolan could have gotten a wound like that.

Nolan glanced at him, a smirk morphing on his face. "You can ask. I'm not as sensitive about it as I once was."

"I wouldn't presume. We've just met."

Nolan shrugged and tossed his now-blackened sponge into the garbage bag. "Car accident."

The matter-of-fact way Nolan said the words, there was a large unspoken story to go with them. "I'm glad you made it out okay."

"Mostly." Nolan grabbed another sponge. "The scars people can't see are worse than anything on my body. Those are finally starting to get better too."

Justin didn't need to have been in a car accident to get that emotional wounds tended to be worse than physical ones. "A damaged psyche can take its toll on a person."

"You look like someone who'd get that." Nolan had his back to him, so he didn't see Justin's mouth fall open in surprise. "Zack's better about things now, but it took him a while to understand my challenges." Before Justin had a chance to say anything, Nolan's phone rang. "Hello?"

Nolan stepped outside into the hall, leaving Justin alone with his confusion.

Nolan's words didn't sit right with him. How did he look like someone who would understand a damaged psyche? Justin didn't have any emotional hidden scars. Sure, he might not have had the closest relationship with his parents, but neither had he been abused or completely neglected. Emotionally damaged? No.

Well, not really.

Nolan came back into the apartment, eyes wide. "Ah, I have to bail on you. I'm sorry."

"Problem?"

"My volunteer coordinator for the speed dating event just backed out on me. I need to make some calls and try to find someone. Fast."

Maybe his time away from working with the Barnes family had softened Justin. A few years ago, he wouldn't have thought twice about Nolan's predicament. It wasn't his business; therefore, he would simply have kept the hell out of it. But he had a place to stay and a job because of Zack and Nolan, and it was the least he could do to offer up his meager services for a few hours.

Besides, if he was *working* the speed dating event, he couldn't *participate* in the speed dating event. Poor Grady would lose his little bet and have to suffer the consequences of his hubris. "If you need an organizer, I can certainly assist. I don't have any other plans, and I'll probably need fresh air after being in this place for a few days."

"Would you?" Nolan's smile brightened. "You're my new best friend. Okay, yes. I'll get the information together and have it ready for you. I'll really have to get you a shirt now. I'll let Zack know." Nolan's brain was visibly spinning. "Yeah, this will work."

"Let me know when to show up and I'll be there. Thanks for the help today."

"Of course. You know where to find me if you ever need anything. Zack likes to think he's in charge, but . . ." Nolan grinned. "I'll call my plumber as soon as I get downstairs."

As quickly as he'd materialized, Nolan was gone. Justin's cheeks were sore from smiling, something he hadn't realized he'd even been doing. It had felt good to talk to someone whom he didn't have a history with, who didn't have any preconceived notions of who Justin McCormick was, or what he could do. Even when he'd needed something, Nolan hadn't assumed Justin would jump to his rescue, which had made it all the more natural for him to do so.

It was strange. And refreshing.

The sudden appearance of a large spider on the counter he'd just cleaned startled him. Justin picked the spider up so it rested in the palm of his hand. "Not the place for you."

He took it over to the open window and set it on the ledge near a small hole in the screen. The arachnid scampered away to freedom.

Justin had done his own scampering and, for the time being, had settled someplace that gave him hope. Maybe for once, Justin could be selfish and take a small measure of happiness for himself. That wasn't asking too much.

Was it?

═ CHAPTER ═
FIVE

The moment Finn set foot into Ringside Gym, he knew he'd made a mistake agreeing to come to the speed dating event. For all the time he'd been coming here, this was the most people he'd ever seen present at once. Men and women mingled, talking and laughing so loud that it echoed in the large open room. There was an energy in the air, something that Finn could feel against his skin.

Devan's eyes widened as he, Eli, and Finn walked over to the registration table. "This is crazy."

"Aren't you sorry you volunteered us to help out now?" Eli's smile made his eyes sparkle. "That'll teach you to be all noble and stuff."

"We owe them." Devan turned to Finn and smiled. "You better get registered while we figure out where Nolan needs us to be."

Finn's heart was pounding, though whether from fear or excitement, he couldn't be certain. "Yup. Probably won't stay for the whole event, so don't worry if you can't find me."

The couple shared a look before Finn walked past them. He'd held up his end of their agreement, so what if he only sat through one or two of these things before bailing. The money was going to a good cause, and that was the important part.

The registration line moved quickly, and before he knew it, Finn was face-to-face with the new guy he'd met the other day. Jason or Jessie . . . or something. Finn tried to see if the man had a name tag on, which, nope, of course he didn't. *Wonderful.*

Finn swallowed, and his lips trembled as he forced a smile. "Ah, hi." A blush heated his cheeks the moment the guy met his gaze. The dark-rimmed glasses gave him the appearance of a stern teacher, which was attraction catnip for Finn.

The man smiled, but it didn't quite reach his eyes. "Finn, correct?" He looked down the list in front of him. "There you are, Finn Miller."

If Finn had been a bit embarrassed before, knowing that this attractive man remembered him from their brief meeting was downright mortifying. "Ah, yup. That's me."

"Here's your name tag, an explanation of the evening's events, and your date rating card." He pushed his glasses up his nose. "Things are about to get started, so you might want to head over to the ring."

"Justin, how many more in your line?" Nolan called out from somewhere unseen.

Justin! Right.

Taking his package, Finn put his name tag on and headed to the gathering crowd. Even though Nolan had been promoting the event a lot at the gym, there appeared to be a large number of people who weren't members. Fresh faces, unknown quantities, and no way for Finn to adequately prep.

What the hell am I doing here?

Zack climbed up onto the boxing ring and clapped his hands. "Hello everyone. Welcome to Ringside Gym and our first annual speed dating event. All proceeds will be going to launch our LGBTQ after-school self-defense class. If you'd like more information on the classes, or if you know a youth who might benefit from attending, please speak with Nolan. He's the cute one hiding in the office." Zack smiled and waved in that direction.

Finn tried to look around, but every time he made eye contact with someone, his gaze would drop to the floor as if his eyeballs were weighted. He shifted until he was toward the back of the crowd, then he bumped into someone. "Sorry."

The remainder of his apology died in his throat when he realized he'd practically stepped on Leo, who smiled and winked at Finn. "It's all good, handsome."

Oh God, oh God. He should say something else, *anything* else as to not come across as a complete idiot. But Leo had already turned his gaze back to Zack, who was explaining how the evening was going to work based on sexuality self-identification. Finn barely recognized the words as English.

"If you have a blue name tag, that means you're sitting at the tables in the yoga room." Zack pointed to Eli. "You can follow the attractive bald man, and he'll take you up. Everyone else, stay here for a moment, and then I'll let you know where to go next."

Leo leaned in toward Finn, tapped his blue name tag, and purred, "That's us."

Finn didn't know how he was going to make it all the way to the yoga studio sporting a massive boner and not be made fun of. Holding the card in front of his pants, he mentally went through every disgusting image he could dredge up in order to help deflate his bulge. Not that it was working with Leo wearing tight jeans and walking in front of him.

God, life totally wasn't fair at times.

Once they made it to the studio, they were filtered out once more. Eli stood at the doorway, playing traffic cop. "If there's an *A* on your name tag in the bottom corner, you're at a table. *B* and you're going to be the one on the move."

Thankfully, Finn was an A, which meant he'd have the blessed table as cover. He found the closest available one and fell into the chair. Why the hell had he agreed to this? Never again.

Eli clapped his hands. "I think I'm supposed to say something inspiring." He shrugged. "No one died from participating in one of these events. Just have fun." His gaze landed on Finn for a moment. "When you hear the bell, you have eight minutes to spend with your date. When the bell goes off again, you'll move clockwise to the next table."

The bell went off, and before Finn had a second to catch his breath, a man sat down across from him.

"Hi there, I'm Jordan." He held out his hand, and Finn took it without thinking.

"Finn." Woohoo, he'd managed to get a whole word out.

Jordan was dark-skinned, with the richest brown eyes Finn had ever seen. There was something easygoing in his smile that should have set Finn at ease. Instead, his heart pounded and he had to wipe his hands on his jeans.

Jordan cleared his throat. "I'm a business student, graduating this year. I've been out since I was sixteen, and I'm looking for someone not only to date, but someone who would like to go on some adventures with me. Like," he scooted forward in his chair, "going to one of those escape-room things. The whole idea of using our wits to figure out the clues sounds like so much fun."

Finn forced his gaze to stay up and locked on Jordan's. He managed to smile and nod. Jordan frowned. "Is that something you might be interested in doing?"

Shit, he had to speak. "Ah. Maybe."

Jordan smiled, but not as brightly as before. "There are a lot of different types. Horror themed, mystery, and even espionage ones. I haven't gone before, but it's on my list to do this summer."

Finn squeezed his legs. "It sounds fun."

"What about you? What do you like to do?"

Okay. He'd been asked a straightforward question. Finn could manage to talk about what he liked. He managed a wobbly smile. "I'm a tech guy. I play video games and . . . ah, read."

There. Those were words that comprised a sentence. It even made sense! Finn smiled and basked in the glow of his success.

Jordan leaned back in his seat. "So, you're kind of a stay-at-home guy."

"I guess." Was he? He liked going out to movies and to art shows, though he always felt weird going alone. He'd probably do more of those things if he had someone willing to go with him. Maybe someone like Jordan.

Then the bell chimed and Jordan was out of his chair before Finn had a chance to say goodbye.

The wee bit of excitement he'd felt vaporized. This wasn't who he was as a person. He didn't do nanosecond first impressions really well, never had. Why he'd thought tonight would be any different, he didn't have a fucking clue.

Another man had taken Jordan's place. He held out his hand and smiled. "Hi, I'm Scott."

Finn did his best to push past his previous failure and start again. "Finn. Nice to meet you."

They then proceeded to spend most of the eight minutes awkwardly staring at one another and attempting small talk.

Ding. Switch.

"Hi, I'm Palmer."

Ding. Switch.

"Hi, I'm Malik."

Ding. Switch.

With each passing person, Finn found it harder and harder to look the person across from him in the eye. How the hell did people do this? Figure out what to say in a split second and not sound like a complete idiot? That was clearly a skill that he hadn't been born with, and he'd never managed to learn it.

Fuck it, he was leaving.

Finn was halfway out of his chair when Leo sat down across from him. It was as though Finn's ass had a magnet implanted in it; he plopped back down onto the metal folding chair. If Leo had been aware of his actions, he certainly didn't acknowledge them.

"Hello, handsome." Leo stuck out his hand. "Leo Hayes. I've seen you around, haven't I?"

Holy shit, Leo knew who he was. "Ah yeah. I train with Eli."

"Yes, that's it. I've seen you in the ring more than once. Man, he must be brutal to work with. I've only sparred with him once, but he handed me my ass."

I'd like to handle your ass. "He does that."

Leo leaned back in his chair and half turned his body, presumably so he could keep his gaze moving around the room. "He's on my wish list of people to beat. I mean, it will probably never happen, but a man's got to have goals, am I right?"

"Yup." God, he had the most attractive neck Finn had ever seen on another human being. Who knew that necks could be such a turn on?

"I'm not sure about this whole speed dating thing. I wasn't going to come, but then the guys guilted me into it. Figured that if people knew I was coming, they might get a few more attendees." He leaned forward just enough that Finn caught a flash of the chest tattoo beneath his shirt. "Apparently, I have a few groupies around here. Isn't that fucking hilarious?"

I'm your groupie. I'll do whatever you want. "Yeah."

Leo cocked his head to the side and smiled. "I like you. What did you say your name was again?"

"Finn."

"So, Finn, have you had better luck than me tonight? Maybe my standards are too high, but every time I sit down at a table, I just get a feeling of dread." He winked. "Except with you."

Words. I have to use my fucking words. "Not yet."

Leo slapped his hand on the table. "Awesome. I would have felt like a complete asshole if I was the only picky bastard here. Nice to know I'm in good company."

Ding.

Finn's heart raced as Leo let out a big sigh. "I guess that means I need to be on my way."

"Want to go out on a date?"

Finn froze the moment he realized that the words had come from his own mouth. He hadn't just done that. Had he?

Leo's grin widened. "Sounds like a plan. I'll mark you on my card, and we can exchange information." And rather than only *say* he was going to do that, he placed his card on the table in front of Finn and made the mark so Finn could see it. He waited for Finn to follow suit. "Awesome. I'll see you soon."

As Leo moved away, Eli clapped his hands. "Okay, everyone. Let's take a fifteen-minute break. There's coffee, tea, energy drinks, and snacks in the back of the room. We also have baked goods from the Pear Tree around the corner."

Finn's hands shook as he reached for the table edge. He felt as though he'd run a marathon while hopped up on Red Bull. He was going on a date with Leo! This was possibly the best thing in the world that could have happened to him.

Or the worst.

Because going on a date with Leo meant actually having a conversation with Leo. And if tonight was anything to go by, the chances of him going on a *second* date with Leo would be next to none.

Shit, this was going to be a disaster.

Someone sat down opposite him. Finn had to blink when he realized it was Justin. Wearing a baggy Ringside T-shirt that didn't suit him at all and sporting what could only be classified as a frown.

"You're going on a date with . . . that man." Justin motioned over to the refreshment table where Leo was currently laughing with a small group.

"How did you—"

"I was standing right there." He pointed to a spot a few feet away from Finn's table. "Hard not to hear."

"Oh." Finn must have been really excited not to have noticed Justin. The man's air of annoyance alone would normally be enough to put his hackles on edge. "Yeah, we are."

"Is that something you wanted? Did he pressure you into the date?" There was genuine concern in Justin's voice. Strange, given they'd only talked twice before.

"It is. I asked him."

"Honestly?" Justin crossed his arms. "You looked terrified once he left. I wanted to check in and make sure everything was okay."

Finn stared into his eyes, and a dam broke inside him. "I've had a . . . God, saying 'a crush' makes me sound like a kid, but I've had a crush on Leo for a while now. I don't do well with people or with conversations. Tonight has pretty much been an intense version of Hell for me. But when he was going to leave I . . . I couldn't let that happen." The burst of energy left him once again. "I just don't think I'm going to be able to have a conversation with him for longer than eight minutes."

"You seem to have no problems talking to me."

Finn blinked, as the reality of Justin's words hit him. "Oh."

Justin narrowed his gaze. "Why do you think that is?"

"I . . . well. You're, ah, different? I don't want to date you?" Finn straightened. "No offense." God, this was the worst.

Justin waved him away. "You need a coach. Someone who can help you learn the finer art of conversation."

God, that sounded exactly like what he needed. "That would be amazing. I can't imagine anyone wanting to take me on for something that tedious though."

Justin nodded twice. The first appeared to be to himself, but the second time he made direct eye contact with Finn. "Agreed."

"Agreed . . . to what? Me being tedious?"

"To me being your conversation coach."

CHAPTER SIX

Justin had spent the better part of the first hour of the speed dating event watching Finn face-plant every time a new man sat down at his table. At first, he'd been surprised at how nervous Finn was. Public speaking was a personal strength, and he'd mastered the art of small talk by the time he was ten. Yes, he was well aware that not everyone was particularly skilled, or even cared about perfecting social niceties. But watching someone else struggle so obviously, someone who kept trying but failing to make a go of it, had made Justin more than a little embarrassed for the man. With each subsequent date, Justin had gotten a few steps closer to Finn, silently encouraging him on, only to cringe when Finn inevitably stumbled and his "date" shut down.

He'd been about to step in, to maybe offer a few pointers, when the blond sat down at Finn's table. Gone had been the awkward man, and in a snap, he'd been replaced with someone who was most definitely in love—or at the very least in lust. Justin moved close enough to catch most of the conversation. Well, what little of it there was. Leo was self-indulgently talking so much, it was a wonder Finn hadn't bonked him over the head with something.

He'd have heard the end of the conversation if it hadn't been for Eli informing him of the impending break. When Justin had turned back around to see how Finn was doing, Leo had been in the process of arranging a date.

None of this particularly mattered to Justin. He didn't know either man, or what their past relationship was, if anything. And as Grady would have pointed out if he were here, it was none of his goddamned business what was going on between the two men.

Still . . .

While he'd only been in town a week, he'd spent the bulk of that time at Ringside, so he'd seen Finn multiple times in the days since their awkward introduction. Finn rarely spoke to anyone beyond Eli; he appeared to be quite competent when it came to fighting, and when he wasn't looking at the heavy bag, he was staring at Leo. Justin couldn't help but feel sorry for Finn, knowing that he had feelings for a man who didn't seem to know he existed.

Finn licked his lips, and his gaze slipped to the table. While others in the room were laughing and carrying on, Justin sat there, knowing that, any moment, Finn would have his words organized.

Finn finally met his gaze. "Why would you want to help me? It's not like we're friends."

Justin smiled in that way he used to do to drive Grady crazy. "I've been told in the past that I'm not the nicest of men. It's part of the reason I moved to Toronto in the first place." It was his turn to look away. "Consider you doing me a favor. An opportunity to redeem myself."

"What do you need to redeem yourself from?"

"As I said, I'm a bit of an asshole."

Finn chuckled. "You don't strike me as one."

"You haven't known me long enough. I guarantee by the end of this little project, two things will be true. One, I'll have you conversing like a prize-winning orator. And second, you'll probably want nothing more to do with me."

Justin half expected Finn to stand up and get the hell out of there at this point. Instead, he cocked his head and smiled. "I guess I can't claim you didn't warn me."

Finn held his hand out. Justin responded in kind, almost as a reflex. The slide of skin on skin drew a tingle up the middle of Justin's spine. Strange, he almost never reacted that way. Letting the handshake go on a tad longer than normal, Justin finally pulled away. "Excellent."

"Does this mean I can skip the rest of tonight's thing?" Finn's body relaxed, and his head dipped lower. "I never knew trying to do so much small talk could be this draining."

Maybe it was because Finn didn't know Justin, that his tone was one of relief and comradery. Maybe he was exhausted and for a moment his guard had dropped. Whatever it was, when Finn looked back up at him, Justin would have done anything to save him from further harm.

"I could use some help." He stood up just as Eli was letting people at the food station know that they were about to get started again. "Come on."

Finn's grin could have powered a small building for a year. "Awesome."

Eli saw them coming, and the look on his face was one of approval. "Hey, Finn. How's your night been going so far?"

Finn shrugged. "I have a date."

"Really? That's awesome. Devan will be so happy to hear that." Eli smiled as he squeezed Finn's shoulder.

"I'm going to steal him for a while." Justin couldn't help but straighten when Eli's gaze narrowed on him. He really was quite intimidating. "With his permission."

"I'm done in." Finn stepped closer to Justin, which helped ease Justin's tension. "I figure I can help out a bit rather than bail completely."

"Sure. Have at it." Eli clapped his hands as he walked away. "Okay, everyone. Time to get going. We're going to shuffle people around, so you get to meet as many different people as you can. And it looks like we'll have one empty spot, which will mean one empty table per round."

Finn began to check the coffee urns. "Thanks again. I don't think I could have handled much more of that."

Justin started picking up the abandoned coffee cups, napkins, and sugar packets. "It looked painful for you. But we can work on that. You're a natural once you're relaxed."

Without saying much else, they fell into a rhythm, cleaning the mess as the chatter of voices echoed behind them. It felt strange having someone at his side to help, even for something this small. Justin had become a solitary person mostly out of necessity. It was normally easier, faster for him to do things on his own. When Grady had been younger, he'd tried to get him to help, wanting to treat him as a friend. But the animosity that had grown between them had made it impossible for that to continue. So, Justin had gone it alone.

"You've just moved to Toronto?"

He started at the closeness of Finn's voice next to him. Justin pushed his glasses up his nose. "I have. I'm from Vancouver originally."

"I've never been. I've heard it's nice out there." Finn reached across Justin, their arms brushing.

Justin had to take a breath. Finn was cute, but far too clueless for that to have been anything other than accidental. "Mountains and ocean. You really can't beat it."

"I haven't gone farther west than Stratford. School trip to go see the Shakespeare festival one spring. I nearly threw up on the bus."

Justin barely stopped himself from smiling. He could picture Finn, probably scrawny, definitely geeky, sitting in the middle of a noisy school bus, trying to keep his shit together. "Charming."

"They did *Hamlet*. I don't remember who any of the actors were, but the lead had this voice . . . deep and commanding and way sexy, that had me riveted." Finn stopped and looked at him. "Actually, your voice sounds a bit like his."

Justin cleared his throat and hoped he wasn't reading too much into Finn's words. "Let's get these things downstairs."

They walked down the stairs to the small kitchenette that the gym staff used for their lunches. Justin had laid claim earlier that morning for the first time, thankful there was a microwave he could use. Cooking wasn't a skill he'd mastered in his life. Far better to let someone else cook the meals.

"Apparently, they have someone who comes in and cleans the kitchen. I was told all we have to do is put any dishes in the sink." Justin did exactly that.

"Why not put them in the dishwasher? It's right . . . you know. There."

Justin had asked the same thing. "Nolan said it has to do with their contract. I'm here on their good graces, so I don't want to be doing anything that will cause them problems."

"What do you mean? You're not living at the gym, are you?"

"Hardly. Upstairs. I'm working on a project for Zack. We're going to be converting the apartments upstairs into executive suites."

Finn's frown deepened. "I didn't even know there was anything above the yoga studio. Well . . . yes, I did, but not that Zack owned it or that it wasn't already occupied."

"It's phase three of what Nolan is calling their master plan." Justin wasn't sure if it was meant to be a diabolical plan or not, but given how much grinning Nolan tended to do when talking about the future, Justin had no doubt that it was. "I'm helping them with the development side, given how busy they both are with the gym."

"Huh." Finn finished sorting the recycling. "Let me know if you need help. I can run cable for any tech stuff, and I'm pretty handy when it comes to carpentry. It's the least I can do if you're going to help me with my Leo problem."

Justin paused but kept his gaze averted. It was strange how Finn had no issues speaking to him, when he'd clearly been struggling only a short time earlier. It shouldn't be that hard to help him, and if it meant he had the added bonus of some company, then he had nothing to lose. "When are you free for your first lesson?"

Finn's face was beet red when Justin glanced over. "Ah . . . well . . . tomorrow?"

Maybe not quite as relaxed as Justin had assumed. "Come to my place. Or what little there is of it. Better to use the interior stairwell for now. Right over there." He pointed to the large steel door across from the kitchen. "We need to replace the exterior doors and fix up the security gates, so it's not exactly safe on the outside yet." His hand came close to Finn's shoulder, and Justin could almost feel the tension radiating from him. "Seven o'clock work?"

Finn nodded.

It didn't take a genius to realize Finn had reached his conversation capacity for the evening. "If you're looking to escape, this is probably the best time. I'll tell Eli where you've gone."

Finn's shoulders dropped. "Thank you. I'll cab it."

"I'll let him know." Finn hesitated to leave, and Justin could imagine what was going on in his brain. "If you want to bail on the lessons at any time, simply don't come. I won't be offended."

"Okay. Thanks." Finn continued to hesitate for a minute, tapped the counter with his fingertip, and then bolted.

Justin wasn't sure if he felt sorry for Finn and his social awkwardness, or admiration for him doing his best to push his boundaries. Justin wasn't normally one for putting himself out there, not when there was a chance he wouldn't come out on top. He was social and a shrewd negotiator, but he'd gotten there through years of crafting his persona, learning how to manipulate the situation to what he wanted it to be. His exterior was polished, practiced, and in no way designed to let anyone in.

Nothing good ever came of that.

So yes, if Finn showed up tomorrow night, he'd help him build up the wall Finn would need to be able to put himself out there, to make it so no matter how he felt on the inside, no one would see the turmoil. Justin was an expert on that, after all.

CHAPTER SEVEN

E xhaustion warred with fear as Finn walked through Ringside on his way to the door Justin had pointed out last night. He hadn't slept well, spending the majority of the time tossing and turning, which had only served to piss King off. Eventually, the dog had left him with a low growl and had gone to sleep on the couch.

Finn's thoughts had shifted all night from Leo's smiling face, to Justin's offer of help. Both things should bring him joy: a date with the man he'd been obsessing over for months now, and the opportunity to learn how to not make a complete ass of himself in public on a daily basis.

Naturally, that meant both terrified him.

At least with Justin, Finn hadn't felt the need to say everything exactly right. Unlike a lot of other people, Justin didn't rush him or fill the silences when Finn was trying to find the right words to say. It was as though the pressure had been relieved, if only temporarily, in the short time they'd talked.

That hadn't made coming here any easier. If anything, Finn had nearly taken Justin up on his offer to bail, no questions asked. But instead, he'd grabbed a box of network cable and his fisher, and left before he could talk himself out of it.

Because regardless of what he constantly told his parents—and even himself—the truth of the matter was that he *was* lonely and wanted nothing more than to find a way to win Leo over. He wanted to spend evenings smiling and laughing, talking about boxing and computer games. He wanted to find out what it would be like to kiss Leo, to feel that joy and exuberance pressed against his skin. If he had to spend time with a man who seemed to have no joy in him at all to get there, then that was what he'd do.

The stairway was too dark, and the wood on the stairs was going to need to be refinished. When he made it to the third floor, he paused. Justin hadn't said which apartment he was staying in, and considering the long hallway of closed doors to choose from, this wasn't exactly going to be a quick search.

"Shit!"

Or maybe it would be.

He walked over to the door where Justin's shout had come from and tapped on it. It took a minute, and when Justin opened up, Finn couldn't help but smile; Justin was filthy, the complete opposite of the well-put-together man who'd been at the event last evening. "Catch you at a bad time?"

Justin's lips were a tight line, but after a moment he seemed to relax. "I'm glad you came. It seems I need someone to save me from myself tonight."

As Finn entered the apartment, he was surprised by the unusual smell. He was equally shocked at the array of started projects around the room: countertops that were half torn apart, cupboard doors opened and shelves removed, and the sink faucet was off. "Ah, a little renovation?"

Justin pushed at the bridge of his glasses. "The plumber came in today, which derailed my other attempts at making this place less repugnant. The smell I'm sure you've noticed is apparently something do to with the pipes, mold, and possibly a dead creature somewhere in a wall."

Finn didn't know Justin at all, but he didn't seem to be the type of man to handle less-than-stellar living accommodations. "My dad's a carpenter. I can help with the kitchen if you'd like."

Justin's gaze snapped to his, and it felt as though he were looking past Finn's eyes and directly into his brain. "I don't have tools. Not the proper ones in any case. I was planning on hiring a professional. But given how long it's going to take to get a contractor in here, I'll have to do a few of the minor tasks myself to make this place livable in the meantime."

"Sure. Okay. Yeah, that's important. Ah. I can't do a lot but . . . I can help. A little." He lifted up the box. "I can get the place ready for internet."

That brought a small smile to Justin's face, which helped ease Finn's nerves. "That would be beneficial. Zack swore that his wi-fi would work up here, but it doesn't. My data charges are going to kill me, and if I don't have access to at least Netflix, I'm going to lose my mind. It's far too quiet here at night."

Finn relaxed further. The overwhelming silence that had filled his apartment was the worst thing about living alone. It was one of the reasons he'd gone out and gotten King. It was good to know he would be able to help Justin. "I can get you all fixed up. I didn't know if you'd need anything, but I have a router as well and can see about calling Rogers and getting you some high-speed, if you want."

Justin blinked at him. "Those are words that mean I'll get my email and be able to watch movies, yes?"

"Yes." Finn smiled but couldn't help averting his gaze when he felt a blush cross his face. "I'll start."

It wasn't as easy to ignore Justin as it was other clients. Usually, once he started hauling out cable and equipment, most people would wander away, bored in minutes. Being ignored helped him fall into his troubleshooting pattern and get everything done that he'd need to.

But Finn was constantly aware of Justin's presence. He could feel Justin's gaze on him as he moved around the apartment, tapping on walls and checking out the small spaces he could use alongside the heating vents to run the cable. It was as though Justin was somehow touching his body with that assessing look—a caress far gentler than the man who wielded it.

"Are you a coffee drinker?" Justin's voice had a way of filling the entire room without him yelling. "I've managed to keep a steady supply brewed without blowing a fuse."

God, there's something about his voice . . . "Yeah. Black. Please."

"You should stop doing that."

Finn looked up; no doubt his eyes were owl-wide. "What?"

Justin was pouring two mugs of coffee. "Try and hide when you're speaking to someone. You tend to turn away, speak your words to the floor or the wall. I assume you're trying to not put yourself in the center of attention."

Do I? "I didn't realize."

"Not surprising." Justin strode over to him and stopped a foot away, holding out the mug for him to take. "Most people who are nervous speaking or have a certain amount of social anxiety will do what they can to avoid what they consider emotional danger."

Being on his knees, Finn had no choice but to look up at Justin to accept the coffee. Justin might not be a huge man physically—he was actually a few inches shorter than Finn—but he had *presence*. He was a bit like Leo that way. "Yeah. I do that."

"You also are quite chatty when you're not worried about making an impression."

The mug was hot as Finn gripped it. The pain was a good distraction from the pounding in his chest and the tightening in his groin. "I don't think I've ever been called 'chatty.' Ever. In my entire life."

"Stand up. I want to try something." Justin took a step back, giving him space.

Finn swallowed down a burning sip of coffee, before setting the mug on the floor and doing what Justin had asked. Now facing one another, it was even harder for him to meet Justin's gaze. How screwed up was he that last night he'd practically poured his soul out to this man, but now that he knew him a bit better, his embarrassment threatened to press him down?

Because his gaze was pointed at the floor, it was easy for Finn to see when Justin stuck his hand out. "Hello. My name is Justin McCormick."

When Finn managed to look up at him, he was relieved to see that Justin's expression wasn't patronizing, condescending, or amused. Justin didn't move, and his steady hand didn't waver. Finn cleared his throat and straightened, before reaching out to take Justin's hand in a firm shake.

"Hi. I'm Finn Miller. Nice to meet you."

Justin gave his hand a tiny squeeze, which sent a shiver through Finn, before letting it go. "Nice to meet you as well. I don't think you told me what you do for a living."

"Ah . . ." Hadn't he? Finn tried to go back and replay their previous conversations. "Sorry. I'm a computer network engineer. I work for a data security company and do on-site and phone support for our clients."

Justin nodded. "Good. First pointer for you: There are several basic questions that we all tend to get asked in social situations. Who we are. What we do professionally. What we do for hobbies. It takes some of the stress out of those small-talk situations if you've practiced out loud what you're going to say."

That . . . made a surprising amount of sense. "I can do that. I live home alone with my dog. I'll practice on him."

"Consider that your first lesson. The next time we meet, I'm going to introduce myself again and we'll have an ice-breaker chat." Justin nodded, took a sip of his coffee, and went back to the kitchen. "Now, I need to figure out how much bleach is safe to use on every surface here."

Finn watched him, fascinated by how quickly Justin seemed to change from being personable, to having this wall erected around him. He knew it was a wall, because he'd been looking out over the top of his own since he was a teen. Walls kept him safe. Which meant Justin felt he had something that he needed to be kept safe from as well. It struck Finn as strange to think of this confident man needing protection from anything. Or anyone.

Doing his best to ignore Justin, Finn started running cables through the walls to where he thought would be the best place for the modem. It took more physical effort than most people realized to do this part of the job. The image of the out-of-shape tech geek, forever placed in front of a computer screen wasn't as real as television shows portrayed. Well, at least not when it came to racking servers and running cable.

Sweat rose on his body as his muscles ached slightly from the effort and concentration it took to force his fisher through spaces it didn't want to go. When he stood up, a solid forty minutes later, and brushed off his hands, he was surprised to see Justin openly staring at him. "What?"

"I've never seen anyone do that. The techs at the company I worked for would scurry away whenever they saw people coming." Justin cocked his head to the side. "It was interesting."

Finn was immediately aware of the stink that now clung to him, and the dirt that inevitably covered his jeans and T-shirt from crawling around the dingy apartment. He needed a shower, to get some fresh air, and to wrap his head around his first lesson. "It'll do for now. It's not the fastest you can get, but it'll get you the basics until the cable company can come. When your building contractor comes, I can rerun this so the cables are better hidden and protected. I can also run audio cable and install in-ceiling speakers, but both the walls need to be opened up for me to do that properly. If you're looking to add some wow factor to these apartments, then that's the way to do it."

Justin's eyes narrowed. "You talk just fine when you go all techie."

Do I? Finn shrugged. "It's stuff I know. No one really pays attention. Eyes glaze over, that sort of thing." He took a shuffle step toward the door, but hesitated. "Did you ever have that happen to you?"

Justin straightened. Ah, there was that annoyance Finn had seen back at the gym the first day they'd met. "Never."

And just like that, the small flutter of attraction he'd felt for Justin snuffed itself out. "You're lucky." The muscles in his chest tightened, amping up his need to flee. "I better go." Without waiting for permission, Finn quickly grabbed his tools and headed for the door.

"You can back out at any time."

Justin's words stopped him dead in his tracks. Finn turned back around. "What?"

"Our agreement." Justin had laced his fingers behind his back and stood rigid enough to look natural in a military parade. "You're under no obligation to come back."

Finn nodded, but wasn't entirely certain what he was agreeing to.

"I'm not the easiest person in the world to tolerate. I'm not oblivious to my failings, and I don't take another person's rejection of those aspects of me personally." Justin's gaze didn't waver; his eyes were wide and unblinking. "My feelings can't be hurt."

I somehow doubt that. For once Finn didn't overthink matters, and reached into his pocket. "Here's my business card. It has my email address. We can work out another meeting."

And that simple act used up the last of his social energy. With a quirky smile, he left.

CHAPTER EIGHT

One Week Later

Justin stood in Zack's office, arms crossed and frustration on full display. He'd been at this project for under two weeks and he was ready to pack up his few belongings and move back to Vancouver with his tail between his legs. Really, it shouldn't be this difficult to arrange for the renovation of a single apartment.

The current thorn that had been shoved deep into his side was the need to rewire the entire place, including the installation of an upgraded electrical panel. He wasn't an electrician, and had very little interest in what the tradespeople needed to do beyond getting their jobs completed on time and under budget.

Nolan sat behind the desk, staring intently at an Excel spreadsheet, while said electrician sat opposite him. "Okay, so we need a panel surge protector?"

"If you have anyone in there with high-end electronics, you want to make sure their stuff is protected. Especially if they're renting from you. It's something I recommend for most home owners and all renters."

Nolan somehow leaned even closer to the screen. "That wasn't in your initial estimate."

"No, but given what I saw upstairs, I would recommend it for each apartment unit. Trust me, it's cheaper than the insurance costs if you have to cover damage."

The contractor had refused to listen to Justin's concerns about the cost, and requested a meeting with either Zack or Nolan to confirm some of the finer details. Since Justin wasn't in charge of the final budget, there wasn't a lot he could do, so here he stood, keeping his opinions to himself.

He looked out at the gym. Even after only a couple of weeks, he was already in sync with the ebbs and flows of Ringside. He recognized most of the regulars, knew when the after-school programs started so he could avoid them, and could identify the little cliques that had formed. The loudest and most obvious was that of Leo Hayes, resident heartthrob and current obsession of Finn.

Justin considered himself a good judge of character, and there was something about Leo that he didn't like. He was too loud, too brash, and far too cocky for his own good. He was the last person Justin would have guessed Finn would be interested in.

And it was Finn's desire to win Leo's heart that had stumped Justin from day one. No two people were less alike than Finn and Leo. Why there was any attraction there at all was beyond him. From the bit Justin had observed, Leo was self-centered, only paying attention to people who were able to do something for him. What Finn possessed that Leo could possibly want was still a mystery to Justin. One that he was determined to get to the bottom of.

"Okay, well, I'll leave the schedule details to Justin, seeing as he's the one living in the apartment." Nolan stood up. "But I think we can swing the extra outlets, upgraded panel, and the surge protector."

Justin turned his attention back to Nolan. "The sooner the better. I'm terrified my coffee maker will cause an explosion."

That elicited the smile and soft chuckle from the other men that he'd planned for. The electrician glanced at his phone. "I can fit you in next Wednesday. You'll be offline for most of the day, maybe longer depending on what we run into when we open up the walls."

Justin nodded, squashing his annoyance at the glacial pace things were progressing at. "Thank you."

He stayed back while Nolan walked the man out, and immediately focused back on Leo, who was currently holding court along the back wall close to the door that led to the change rooms and showers. He had his two cronies with him—whose names Justin had yet to learn—and a few newcomers. They were all looking at Leo as he told some sort of story, leaning in. Justin might not like the man, but he was impressed by Leo's ability to captivate an audience.

One moment the group was laughing at something Leo had said, and the next everyone's attention had shifted to the boxing ring. Leo stepped to the front of the group, his hands flexing at his sides.

Eli had climbed into the ring bare-chested and free of shoes, and stood in the center. Leo watched every move Eli made, no doubt trying to size him up. *Interesting.* It took Justin a moment to realize that the other person in the ring was Finn.

Justin froze, surprised as Finn also pulled off his shirt and tossed it to the floor alongside the ring. He had to be lying about being an IT guy. In Justin's experience, men who worked in front of computers did *not* look like that. Sure, standing next to Eli, Finn wasn't as impressive—not that many men could be, given how much the man worked out—and yet, there was something inherently more appealing to Finn in Justin's eyes.

He was muscular without being overwhelmingly huge. His muscles were leaner, fitting his frame and making him sexually attractive. When Justin added Finn's intellect, it made for a pleasingly complete package.

Not for him, but certainly for some appropriate man.

And the more Justin learned about Leo, the more he'd begun to question whether Leo was that man.

The Ringside members normally didn't stop and stare when someone got into the ring, not even when it was Eli. And yet more than a few had stopped their workouts and conversations to watch Eli and Finn spar. Justin was also riveted as the two of them circled one another. He'd missed talking with Finn, but seeing this side of him was also fascinating.

It had been nearly a week since the speed dating event and his one and only lesson with Finn. He hadn't been entirely surprised when Finn hadn't reached out to him to arrange for another meeting, but part of him had been disappointed. No doubt, Finn had already gone on his date with Leo, taking the brief lesson Justin had given him and run with it. And yes, Justin was certainly curious to know how Finn had made out, but Finn's lack of contact had made it clear that he wasn't interested in Justin being involved.

So, Justin hadn't emailed Finn, hadn't chased him at the gym, nor had he done anything to scare Leo off. Justin was going to keep his nose out of someone else's business and let him live his life.

But that didn't mean he wasn't going to watch Finn in the ring.

Finn was far too pleasant to look at for him to do that.

Eli was currently circling Finn as he adjusted his head guard. "Today I want you to work on your roundhouse kicks. I want you to land at least three while we spar."

Finn nodded as he flexed his fingers.

Eli's grin gave Justin shivers. "Let's do this."

Justin didn't know how MMA fighting worked, hadn't ever seen a match. Honestly, he'd never seen the appeal of watching two men beat the shit out of one another, while frantic crowds cheered them on. But when Eli lunged toward Finn, forcing him to roll out of the way, Justin became drawn to the action and stepped out of the office.

Justin drifted into the main ring area just as Finn suddenly twisted his body around and landed a kick to the side of Eli's arm. The air Justin had been pulling into his lungs got caught somewhere deep in the back of his throat. Finn's expression had been so intense, Justin wouldn't have recognized him as the man who'd been so nervous and gentle at his apartment. A tingle marched down Justin's spine, slowly enough that he thought ants had taken up residence beneath his skin. His dress shirt felt tight as he tried to pull in enough oxygen to stop his head from spinning.

Eli continued to circle Finn, taking a few swings at him before lunging once more, this time wrapping Finn up and sending him crashing to the mat. The crowd cheered him on, as Finn struggled to break free of the hold.

"Come on, Finn," Justin muttered as he moved closer still to the ring.

Finn flipped Eli onto his back and landed a punch to the side of his head. The head guard absorbed most of the blow, but even from this angle, Justin could see that it had caught Eli off guard.

But what little momentum Finn had gained was lost just as fast. Eli used his legs to kick Finn off, jumped to his feet, and landed a kick to the middle of Finn's chest. He went flying and landed hard, flat-backed on the canvas. The crowd lost their minds. Justin forced himself not to check on Finn.

He was fine.

He didn't need Justin.

Another few minutes of Eli having his way with Finn and the sparring was finally done. The whole thing had only lasted about ten minutes, but it had been long enough that Justin felt exhausted. Why the hell did people do that to their bodies?

Leo started clapping and was by Eli's side when he climbed out of the ring. "You're a fucking beast, man. That thing you did to put him on his back was awesome."

Eli nodded at Leo, but quickly turned back to Finn once he'd gotten out of the ring. "The first roundhouse was a solid kick. The last two you telegraphed too much. We'll have to work on your punch combo next time."

Finn opened his mouth, but when his gaze landed on Leo, he simply nodded instead.

"I have to shower and leave. I need to pick Matthew up from the sitter." Eli gave Finn's shoulder a squeeze before heading toward the locker room, pausing as he reached Justin. "Hey."

Justin nodded. "That was quite the show."

"He's really getting good."

"Have you told him that?"

"Daily, but he doesn't seem to believe me." He smiled before making a beeline to the showers.

Leo watched Eli's every move until he was out of sight. "I need to get in the ring with him again." He turned to face Finn. "That move you made to get him off you worked well. I'm going to steal that."

Finn's face flushed as his gaze dropped to the floor. "Sure."

Leo grinned. "Hey, you're the speed dating guy. You never called me."

If Finn's eyes grew any wider, they would pop out of his head. Justin waited all of three seconds to make sure he wasn't going to cut Finn off from stuttering out something, before he stepped up. "Sorry to interrupt."

Leo barely cast a glance at Justin. "Then don't."

How quaint. He thinks he has claws. "But I must. Finn, I know you're in the middle of your workout, but we're having problems with the network cable again. Mind stepping into the office to take a look?"

Justin might not have known Finn well, but his relief was obvious. "Sure."

Finn grabbed his shirt from the floor and marched over to the office; Justin quickly fell into step behind him. The moment he was through the door, he closed it behind them. "Sit and breathe."

Finn fell into the chair where the electrician had been sitting only a short time earlier. "Thanks. I . . ." He shook his head. "I hate this."

Justin hated having an eyeful of half-naked Finn. Well, maybe not *hated*, but it certainly was a distraction he couldn't afford at the moment. Finn had muscles in places Justin would very much like to touch, explore in a far more intimate manner. The smell of sweat and the remnants of cologne filled Justin's head, making it hard to concentrate. Yeah, this wasn't going to work. "You're distracting half-naked."

Finn blushed. "Pardon?"

"Mind putting your shirt on?" Justin was on the verge of having to adjust his cock.

"Shit. Sorry."

Justin shouldn't enjoy Finn's nervous ticks, but he was starting to appreciate them. They softened his edges and helped Justin relax. That was a feat unto itself. "Don't apologize for being attractive. Never for that."

Finn's frown was almost as cute as his blush. "You think I'm attractive?"

Justin rolled his eyes, hoping Finn wouldn't notice his arousal. "Don't get cocky. Now, what happened out there?"

"I choked, the way I always do." Finn settled back into his chair.

Leaning against the closed door, Justin refocused on Finn. "I assumed when I hadn't heard from you that you didn't want another lesson and went on your date."

Finn laughed, but there was no humor in it. "Right. I couldn't even call him."

"What do you mean?"

"I dialed his number and hung up the second I heard him answer." Finn dropped his head into his hands. "I should have called you. I'm never going to manage to go on a date if I can't open my mouth without freaking out."

"You're not freaking out right now." Justin cocked his head. "What's different?"

"I'm not trying to impress you." Finn groaned and shifting back in his seat. "I'm going to die alone."

"I've been told I'm intimidating. If you can talk to me, you can talk to anyone."

Finn glanced up. "You're not intimidating."

Justin waved him away. "I want you to do this. I can't stand to see you following him around the gym with your puppy eyes any longer."

"I don't—"

Justin snorted. "He's going to be here until Eli leaves, then he'll lift weights for twenty minutes. Once Eli walks past, I want you to go out there and arrange your date."

Justin didn't like the part of his brain that was shouting at him about how terrible an idea this was; it could shut up because this wasn't about him or what he wanted. He'd decided Finn was going to be a pet project, so he would make damn sure to do everything in his power to make this a success.

For his part, Finn looked ready to bolt. "I can't just go out there and ask him out."

"You're not doing that at all. You're confirming your plans." There had to be a better way to do this. "Stand up."

Finn did as he was told, and Justin was once again struck by the size of him. He had to swallow down his own sudden rush of nerves. "I want you to go out there and say this. Repeat after me: Hi, Leo."

Finn nodded. "Hi, Leo."

"Sorry about that. I had to get them fixed up."

"Sorry about that. I had to get them fixed up." Finn's shoulders began to relax.

Justin kept their gazes locked and did his best to ignore the annoying tingle that had returned. "I wanted to find out when you might be free for that date."

"I wanted to find out . . . when you might be free for that date."

Justin nodded. "Excellent." He spun Finn around and gave his firm shoulders a little squeeze before shoving him gently toward the door. "Go get him."

Finn nearly tripped as he reached for the door and opened it up in a less than stellar transition. Still, he didn't stop until he got to Leo. Justin watched, doing his best to interpret Finn's body language to get a sense how things were going. It only took a few minutes before Leo turned away and Finn strode back to the office.

The smile on his face was all Justin needed to see. "When's the date?"

"Ah, a week Friday. That gives me some time to practice." The way Finn looked at Justin, his chin lowered and his eyes wide—a child couldn't have done a better job. "That is, if I can still take you up on your offer to help me?"

This will not end well. "Of course. Though I'd suggest we practice at the location you'll be having your date. It'll help you feel comfortable."

Justin tended to be honest with himself, even if he kept certain truths from the rest of the world. Deep down, he knew going out on a pretend date with Finn had very little to do with Finn's need to practice social interaction, and more to do with the overwhelming loneliness he himself had been feeling since he'd moved to Toronto. Despite working for Zack and Nolan, and the offers to come spend time with Grady and Max, Justin had been mostly on his own. He'd had opportunities, but it was his constant role as the third wheel that had worn him down. At least with Finn, he had someone who not only didn't judge him for his past actions, but seemed to want to spend time with him.

Even if he was only using Justin for his skills.

Finn had been quiet for over a minute, making the silence fill the room like a weight. Finn finally looked up. There was something in his smile that set Justin off guard. "I invited him over to my place. I told him that I don't do well in groups, and he agreed to come over. So, I guess that means I'm treating you to supper."

— CHAPTER — NINE

Finn was not normally one to lie. It had been drilled into him from a very young age that above all things, you should always tell the truth, even if it was uncomfortable. That had been part of the reason he hadn't been talkative as a child; he'd been terrified that he was going to accidently tell a lie and get in trouble. So why he'd lied to Justin and told him that Leo was coming over to his place, was a complete mystery to him.

Well . . .

It'd had something to do with the way Justin had looked—not sad exactly, but disappointed—when Finn had walked back from his brief conversation with Leo. He didn't know Justin well, but it didn't take a genius to know that he was probably lonely. The least Finn could do was help Justin out by giving him an evening of company and food.

It had been a while since he'd had the pleasure of making dinner for anyone, so really it was win-win.

Or he hoped it would be. Three days later, he was stuck on a conference call with the head office in Sunnyvale, trying to explain to a bunch of nontechnical people why they couldn't simply move a computer lab to the second floor of a building without getting an engineer to check the structural integrity of the building—*basic fucking physics, people*—while trying to cut salad and get his tuna steaks ready to pan sear.

"I'm sorry, but do you have any idea how much a server rack weighs? That's not including the equipment, cables, or power bus. And has anyone considered where we're going to put the air-conditioning units?"

The knock on his door was nearly swallowed up by the muttering coming through his headset. When he opened the door, Finn stopped breathing for a moment at the sight of Justin standing there.

He'd clearly just shaved, his face free of even the hint of a beard. The dark-blue dress shirt did something crazy to his complexion, somehow making the angles of his face seem more defined than before. And his eyes—they were perfectly framed by his dark-rimmed glasses, highlighting the intelligence Finn knew he had.

Giving his head a shake, Finn beckoned Justin in, while pointing at his headset. "We're going to need at least three units for the amount of equipment going in there. Yes, I'm certain. We have a similar setup here in Toronto. You need at minimum one fail-safe unit."

Justin set a bottle of wine on his countertop, before stopping and taking a quick look around the condo. King padded over to check out the newcomer, and gave Justin a sniff before finding his ball. He sat down and placed it at Justin's feet, waiting expectantly for the inevitable game of fetch.

Finn put his phone on mute. "Justin, meet King. Just a warning, if you throw it, you're committed for a solid fifteen minutes. And please make yourself at home. This is taking longer than I thought."

Justin nodded and proceeded to open the wine before making his way out into the living room. Finn stood in the kitchen and proceeded to watch as King picked up his ball and followed, placing it back at Justin's feet the second he stopped moving. Justin cocked an eyebrow, and gently toed the ball away. King immediately retrieved it, returned it to his feet, and gave Justin a small growl.

Finn put his call on mute again. "You have to throw it. He'll keep bugging you until you give in."

"Really?"

"He's spoiled."

Justin finally threw the ball down the hall, King barked happily and raced after it. The delight on Justin's face as he continued to play fetch with King made the rest of the call more than bearable.

Thankfully, it only took ten minutes for the project team to realize that they were nowhere ready to book the move of the computer lab to the new facility. One less nightmare for Finn to worry about.

Still, his ear ached when he finally took the headset off. "I'm sorry about that."

Justin waved him away. "I've spent enough time in a boardroom to know how that goes. You handled yourself quite well."

Finn's face heated at the compliment. "It's my job. Easy to talk when I know what I'm doing."

"That reminds me." Justin dropped the magazine he'd been looking at and strode over to Finn. When he got close enough for Finn to get another whiff of his cologne, Justin stuck out his hand. "Hello, I'm Justin McCormick."

Finn couldn't help but smile as he took his hand. "Hi, I'm Finn Miller. Pleasure to meet you."

Justin nodded. "So, you're a tech guy. What's that like?"

The change of phrasing threw Finn off a bit, and his practiced words caught in his throat. But Justin gave his hand a small squeeze and surprisingly, the tension faded away. "I like it. I work with servers and help my customers on the phone. Plus, I get to work from home, so that's a bonus."

Justin nodded. "Good job."

It should have been strange standing there holding Justin's hand for as long as he was, but it was just the opposite. There was something comforting about the contact, reassuring. Hell, it was almost arousing, though who'd ever heard of getting turned on by a handshake before?

Stupid.

Finn let his hand fall away, and turned from Justin to head into the kitchen. "I hope you like tuna."

"I hope you like red wine. Though it doesn't exactly go with fish, I think we'll make do." Justin leaned against the edge of the counter. "You did well with that exchange."

"You almost got me with how you asked. I'd practiced the other way so much ..." Finn shook his head. "I'm trained to look for patterns in problems, but small talk was something I could never figure out."

"Why?"

Finn froze. "Pardon?"

"Why could you never figure this out?" Justin's arms were crossed, making his dress shirt pull tight across his chest. "It's been my experience that this sort of problem is rooted in a particular event, or how a person was raised. Given that you're an intelligent man, I would assume you'd know what your problem stemmed from. Once you confront that, everything else will get easier."

The kitchen timer went off, causing Finn to jump and King to let out a bark. "That explanation will need a glass of wine." He hid King's ball in the bedroom, and filled his dish with food. With any luck that would keep him out of trouble long enough for them to enjoy their meal.

"Fine. You plate the food and I'll pour." Justin moved into the kitchen space and grabbed two wineglasses from the hanging rack beneath Finn's cupboards. "Talking about it will be good practice for you."

A sudden onslaught of nerves made Finn question that assessment. "Ah. Okay."

It was fortunate that Justin gave him space and silence, because Finn's brain began to play every negative incident from his teen years on a loop. Every heckle, harsh word, physical attack, no matter how large or small, cycled like a demonic carousel. It took every ounce of concentration to make sure he didn't fuck up the tuna.

He was so focused internally that he didn't realize Justin had taken the cutlery he'd placed on the counter, and set the table. "Oh. Thanks for that."

"The least I can do." Justin sat down opposite him at the table, his gaze focusing on him as he lifted the wineglass to his lips. "That smells amazing."

"Thanks. I made the wasabi aioli myself."

Sitting helped him regain a little of his earlier confidence. He waited for Justin to take his first bite of the tuna. There were many things he'd been hoping for, but the small moan of pleasure was a pleasant surprise. "You missed your calling."

"Can you picture me working as a chef? I can't even watch an episode of anything with Gordon Ramsay in it, let alone work with someone like that. I actually get anxious when Ramsay starts yelling."

Justin took that moment to lick his lips. Finn couldn't help but be fascinated by the tip of his tongue and the moistened trail it left behind on his skin. In a flash, he had a mental image of Justin licking other things. *Shit, what the hell's the matter with me?*

"I imagine you could do just about anything you wanted. With enough proper encouragement and enough time."

"Encouragement was never the issue." His parents had been ecstatic when he'd been selected to be his graduating class's valedictorian. They'd worked with him for weeks on his speech, rehearsing every phrase. Not that it had helped. He rubbed the back of his neck. "Do I have to talk about this?" When he met Justin's gaze once again, he was surprised to see that Justin had been focused on his movements.

Justin's gaze slid back to his, but there was no indication of anything beyond casual friendship. "Of course you don't need to speak about it. I'm not here to pressure you into anything. You asked for help. It's your decision whether or not you want to take it. You can do all or none of what I suggest."

This wasn't something Finn spoke to anyone about. His parents had tried to get him to go to therapy over the years, but he couldn't bring himself to do it. But this back-and-forth wasn't that, right? He was only talking to a friend, someone who wouldn't judge him. He could do this.

Yup, he could.

Finn pushed bits of his tuna around his plate. Anticipation raced through him, like a drug agitating his body. What did it matter if he vocalized these thoughts to Justin? They weren't dating; he barely even knew the man. If Justin walked out of Finn's condo and never came back, it wouldn't disrupt the flow of Finn's life. *Screw it.*

"I'm smart." And wasn't *that* a conceited thing to say out loud? "I was always above the curve when it came to math and science throughout school. I got bullied as a result."

Justin made a noise that could only be described as disgusted. "Children can be monsters."

"I didn't make it any easier for myself. The teachers would ask a question, and the answer would just pop out of my mouth. I aced every test I took. The better I did, the more I got bullied."

The words *got bullied* barely scratched the surface. They didn't describe the horror he'd felt at having three kids hold him down and punch him in the stomach until he couldn't breathe. The terror of having a knife pulled on him, its wielder demanding what little money his parents had given him for lunch. He was thankful daily that he hadn't been in school when Instagram and other social media were a thing. He might not have made it.

Justin had put down his glass and fork and was laser focused on him. "I'm sorry."

Finn couldn't help but laugh. "You didn't do it."

"Still." Justin began to finger the side of his plate. "Something else happened. Didn't it?"

Like when he'd spilled everything to Justin about Leo, the torrent of words flowed from Finn unimpeded. "The school had nominations for valedictorian. There were three of us, the top academic students, and the graduating class had to vote for who they wanted. I didn't really want to do the speech, didn't think I had a chance at it, but somehow I won."

He still remembered the joy he'd had that day coming home from school. His parents had been relieved, thrilled for him. It was as though the hell of his four high school years had been washed away with that simple act of acceptance.

If he'd only known.

Justin got up from his chair and moved it around the table so they sat side by side. "What happened?"

Finn no longer had tears left to spill for the boy he'd once been. The words came out steady as the memories unfolded.

"The speech was supposed to be no longer than seven minutes. I'd written out this perfectly timed script; I'd even managed to make a few jokes about being picked on over the years. I'd practiced in front of a mirror and then my parents. I didn't want to risk screwing something up. What I hadn't counted on was the group of assholes in the front row, or their laser pointer. I didn't realize what was happening at first. I couldn't see, then I stumbled over my words, which drew some snickers. When a teacher confiscated the device, I thought I was okay. Until another one shone on my face. I found out later that there were probably ten or more spread throughout the group. I froze, which drew heckles, then insults and finally laughter. I nearly threw up. Thought I would. So I ran. I didn't even go back to get my diploma. I walked home."

After that, every single time a situation would arise where he'd need to speak to a group, Finn would freeze. As he got older, conversations had become increasingly difficult. By the time he'd graduated from university and had gotten a job, he'd pretty much isolated himself. Being with people, putting himself out there was hard work, and in the end, more painful than being alone.

The slide of Justin's hand on his thigh made him jump. He looked up and into Justin's brown eyes. "No one should have done that to you. You didn't deserve that treatment."

He'd been told the same thing by his parents, the school principal, and someone from the school board. Still, hearing someone who wasn't invested in what had happened repeat the words took some of the pain away. "Thank you."

"I'm determined to help you with this. We'll have you win Leo's heart in no time." Justin swayed closer, and for a moment, Finn thought they might kiss.

Finn's heart was pounding, not out of fear, but from a mix of anticipation and lust. "Leo better appreciate what you're doing for him, because I wouldn't be able to have that date with him without your help."

Justin licked his lips again. "If we do this right, Leo won't even know. You'll talk him into your life in no time."

Finn swallowed his nervousness. "That would be amazing."

He wanted to lean in and press his nose to the side of Justin's throat so he could embed himself in that magnificent scent. He wanted to feel his body against Justin's, to get a sense of what it would be like to be naked beside him.

Jesus, what the hell's wrong with me tonight?

Whatever had passed between them shifted as Justin cleared his throat and moved back. "How about we finish eating and then we can practice some bits of conversation?"

"Sure. Yeah. That'd be good."

Finn needed the few moments it took Justin to shift his seat around once more to get his libido under control. He must be really hard up if he was getting aroused by a man who was doing nothing more than helping him out. Justin wasn't even his type! If he'd realized that being close to Justin tonight was going to do this to him, he would have taken longer in the shower and have jerked off.

Justin finished his wine with a long sip, put the glass down with a soft *thunk*, and straightened. "Shall we get down to business?"

CHAPTER
TEN

J ustin was at a loss. Finn's story had equal parts enraged and saddened him, while surprisingly not leaving him feeling sorry for the man. His own challenged youth might not have been ideal, and while he'd often questioned the love of his mother, he had never once found himself in a position where he hadn't been in complete control. The fact Finn had managed to progress as far as he had in his career, in his life, was a testament to Finn's mettle.

Helping him relax enough to have a conversation with Leo would be easy.

The problem was the idea of Finn wanting to be with Leo at all.

Justin and Finn had moved from the kitchen table to the living room couch, the mostly empty bottle of wine on the floor between them. King trailed along behind them, his so-ugly-it's-cute face damp from the water he'd sloppily lapped up after devouring Finn's leftovers. Justin had never been a dog person, but King appeared to be at least tolerable.

Finn had slowly relaxed the more they'd spoken over supper. Justin couldn't help but feel a measure of attraction for him, enticed by his good nature and handsome features. The soft buzz from the wine helped to take some of the edge off, but any more and Justin would risk his control slipping. He couldn't afford that. "Let's try talking about movies. That's usually a great topic of conversation and a basis for you to compare interests."

"Okay." Finn's gaze slipped over to the giant stack of DVDs piled in the corner of the room. "You could probably tell from my collection that I've got eclectic tastes."

"*Citizen Kane* and *Aliens*. Yes, that had caught my eye." They were strangely two of his favorite movies as well. "What makes a good movie for you?"

Finn's face brightened, something that sent a tingle down Justin's back once again. "I'm big on character development. I don't care about genre particularly. I just need to see that growth from beginning to end. And it doesn't even have to be positive growth. Too many movies these days make those changes artificial. I like to see a character turn dark, make choices they know aren't right, but they feel they need to do it because it's the only way."

"That's one of the reasons I prefer television to movies. It gives them a chance to grow."

"Yes. Exactly." The more excited Finn got about a topic, the more he moved his hands. At the moment, he was reaching for the wine with one while waving a loopy circle in the space between them. "There's so much good television on right now."

It was a joy to simply be chatting with someone about nothing of consequence. To not have to worry about making a serious point that would be acted upon or critical in a business meeting. This was . . . pleasant.

Finn shuffled closer to him on the couch. "What about you?"

Justin blinked. "What about me?"

"You said you like TV. What are some of your favorite shows?" Finn's free hand was now resting on the cushion between them. His long fingers were brushing the fabric in a circular motion that was hypnotic.

"*Orphan Black*." He hadn't seen the last season, but it was high on his list. Not to mention, it was the only thing that came to mind.

"Yeah, that one's awesome." Finn's hand stopped, and Justin finally looked up.

Right into Finn's gaze that was far closer now than it'd been moments before. The tingle had morphed into a full-body shiver as Finn's crystal-blue eyes pierced into his. Shit, he'd had too much wine if he was being this affected by Finn's presence. This wasn't supposed to be about him; he was here to help Finn on his date with Leo.

"How am I doing?" Finn's voice was softer, but no less earnest than it'd been before. "Better?"

"Much." Without being able to stop himself, Justin leaned in to Finn. "You're a wonderful conversationalist when you're relaxed."

"I'll have to make sure I have lots of wine on my date, then." Finn's eyes dipped to Justin's lips. "It seems to help."

Justin wanted nothing more than to close the distance between them, to press his mouth to Finn's and see what the wine would taste like on his mouth. It had been far too long since he'd been with someone to enjoy the mutual exchanging of pleasure. Without looking away, he moved his hand until his fingers brushed Finn's. Their gasp was synchronous.

God, this was such a bad idea when he knew Finn's affections and attention lay somewhere else. But after years of putting everyone else first, Justin wanted to take something for himself. Something small, something that, once Finn moved on and Justin was left alone, he could keep with him.

Without breaking contact with Finn's hand, Justin shifted closer. "There's something else we should practice. So that you're ready."

"What's that?" Finn was moving as well, stopping only a few inches away from Justin.

"I assume you want to seduce Leo." The other man's name tasted foul in his mouth; the idea of Finn being with that ass in any way was enough to make him nauseous.

But when Finn's eyes widened ever so slightly, and his lips parted, Justin couldn't think of anything but wanting to get closer.

Wanting to touch.

Wanting to be . . . everything.

"Ah . . ." Finn couldn't seem to look into his eyes any longer. "Yeah."

"You need to know how to seduce with your words as much as you do with your body." Justin slid his fingers along the back of Finn's hand. "A touch can be a powerful thing, but so can the right phrase."

Finn swallowed. "Like what?"

Justin's body was threatening to betray him, to move on its own, to press against Finn in a way that there'd be no coming back from. *Stop. This isn't supposed to be about you.*

He pulled in a long, slow breath. "Leo strikes me as a man who likes compliments. Who needs them to feel a sense of worth. Start with something basic." He cupped Finn's cheek, rubbing his thumb along the skin beneath Finn's eye. "I've never seen blue eyes that clear before. Like little beacons in a dark place."

Finn's skin flushed beneath his touch. "Really? I . . . ah . . ."

Justin scooted closer. "You don't need to say anything but thank you."

"Thank you."

"Why don't you try it?"

Justin might be good at words, but he'd never been one to handle compliments with ease. Compliments had never been bestowed on him in abundance.

If at all.

He had no idea what Finn would say, no idea if he had any qualities worth complimenting. When Finn didn't immediately speak, he pulled back. "I meant to say, pretend I'm Leo. You need to practice what you'll say to him, so it comes naturally." Of course, Finn wouldn't have anything to say about Justin; they barely knew one another. Barely friends. Justin wasn't exactly one to inspire love notes and lust.

The few inches he'd retreated evaporated as Finn followed him. "What I'd say to Leo?"

There was something off in his voice, though Justin couldn't pinpoint what. "That's why we're here."

Finn slid his hand along the back of the couch, close to Justin's body. His gaze locked on to Justin's so intensely that the words Justin had relied on as his weapon and shield fled his mind. For the first time in his life, Justin was at a loss.

"I'd say, 'You have an amazing smile.'" Finn's voice penetrated Justin, sending little bolts of lust exploding through him. "'It brightens up the room whenever I see it.'"

Justin rarely smiled. No one cared about his joy, his pleasure. Sometimes, he didn't care himself.

"'I can pick out your voice in a crowd, no matter who else is there or how loud things get.'" Finn turned his hand so Justin's fingers were now laced with his. "'It's like I have radar that's focused on only you. I remember your scent long after you've gone. It drives me crazy.'"

Leo. He's talking about Leo. "That's good."

Finn narrowed the distance, until it was almost painful to keep looking into his eyes. "'I want to kiss you. I've dreamed about it.'"

"Yes." Justin let his eyes close for a moment, needing a brief respite from Finn's quiet intensity. "He'll love that."

"Should we practice that as well?" Finn squeezed his fingers. "The kiss?"

No, they shouldn't. Justin should get the hell out of here before things went too far and he was left a broken, discarded toy. Instead, he tilted his head just enough so their mouths lined up. "Nothing worse than an awkward post-kiss moment. Good to rehearse." He traversed the final short, deliciously narrow space between them, and kissed Finn.

Despite his hesitation with words, there was nothing tentative about Finn's actions. He opened his mouth wide, letting his tongue brush across Justin's bottom lip. Neither of them took the kiss deeper, leaving it a nipping exploration. But God, did Justin want more. Wanted to pull Finn in, to press his body against Finn's until they were both a moaning mess. He wanted to be at the center of this man's world, to be on the receiving end of the beautiful intensity that was laser focused on another man.

An undeserving man.

Justin's chest had tightened to the point where he could barely breathe. His cock was hard as stone, and it would only take the slightest of strokes to get himself off. It was too much. He pulled back and turned his face away, looking at their distorted reflections in the window. "That's good."

"Justin . . ."

"If you do exactly that, say exactly that, then the next step of your date with Leo will be to the bedroom."

Finn's hand slipped free. "Maybe I shouldn't have him over."

"Why not?" Justin stood, turning so his arousal wasn't obvious. "What's the point of chasing after a man if not to woo him to your bed? You want him in your life; best to make sure you're compatible in all things."

"I . . . Shit." Finn also stood, rubbing the back of his neck as he began to pace. "I lied to you. He's not coming over here. We're going to a restaurant. I didn't think I could handle two dates out somewhere, so I invited you here."

The rush of passion that had flowed through Justin suddenly bottomed out. "You lied." It shouldn't surprise him; Justin wasn't the target of Finn's affections. What would it matter if he wasn't truthful? It didn't. Not at all. "That's fine. Though you could have simply said it was too much. I'm not doing this for me."

Once again, Justin should have realized he was simply being used as the tool, the means to accomplish the desired end. He'd let his guard down slightly, and this was the end result. Finn, while sweet and attractive, was clearly in love with Leo. While tonight's location might have been under false pretenses, he hadn't been anything less than honest about where his desires lay. That was at least something.

"No, it's not fine." Finn marched over to him and took him by the shoulders. Gone was the timid man from a few moments ago, and back was the confident seducer. "I shouldn't have done that to you, not when you've been nothing but kind and supportive. I'm sorry."

Those were words Justin had never heard associated with himself. "There's no reason to apologize. You need someone to help you rehearse your script. I can do that. I'm good at being what others need. Been told that more than once."

Far too good.

But while he might not be the hero of this particular romance, he wasn't about to let himself become the villain. Best if he left before emotions started to run too high. "Thank you for the meal. You really are a wonderful chef. Goodbye, King."

Not wanting Finn to say anything else, he grabbed his things and left.

CHAPTER ELEVEN

Finn stood in the locker room of Ringside, dressed in his workout clothes, at a loss for what he should do next. Eli was undoubtedly waiting for him to come out and start his warm-up, something that Finn normally didn't mind. But today he knew Leo was out there, because they'd made eye contact as Finn had walked through the gym on his way back here. Leo had even gone so far as to wink at him. Which was completely mind-numbingly surreal.

Then there was Justin.

He was in the main office talking to Zack and someone who Finn assumed was a contractor, given the blueprints he'd caught sight of as he passed. Justin hadn't seen him, which had given Finn the opportunity to stare, if only briefly, at the man who'd so unexpectedly come into his life.

Had it only been a week? Two?

Not that they had anything going on between them. But last evening's pretend date had been stuck on repeat in Finn's mind. His lips still held the warmth of Justin's, his nose still held Justin's scent, and his cock had ached long into the night. Why he'd reacted the way he had to a practical stranger, Finn wasn't certain. Justin was abrupt, more than a little snarky, and not even remotely the type of man Finn would be attracted to. So being unable to get Justin out of his mind, especially when he had a date coming up with Leo, didn't make sense.

Rather than confront him, he now stood in the locker room.

Because that was what he always did when he was being a chicken—avoid.

He paced long enough to know that he was being ridiculous. Justin was a friend, that was it. They'd both gotten caught up in the moment, which was understandable. Nothing had changed in his desires, his want for Leo. If anything, he was more determined to see his date through to the end, if for no other reason than to prove to himself that he could do this. Justin was a nice man and good-looking—well, if Finn was being honest, Justin was pretty damn hot. But that didn't mean that Finn would throw away months of longing to pay attention to the new shiny.

No, he had a plan and he needed to stick to it.

He needed to get out to the ring.

Taking a breath, Finn grabbed his gloves and marched out to the ring. Eli was leaning on the ropes talking to one of the other regulars. He smiled at Finn as he got close. "There he is. I thought you got lost back there."

"Sorry." Finn should give some sort of explanation, but the words wouldn't come. He wasn't about to lie to Eli, but the truth was far too embarrassing. "Warm up?"

Eli narrowed his gaze slightly. "Ten minutes. Use Jacobs Ladder until you drop, then finish with jumping jacks."

God, he hated Jacobs Ladder. "Yup."

The machine was off in the corner, pressed against the wall. The wooden rungs looked easy enough to master—oh hey, nothing more than a perpetual ladder—until you realized that the never-ending hand-over-hand, rung-after-rung climbing sapped the life from you within seconds. It was Eli's favorite torture device.

Today it would be doubly so for Finn, because it gave him an unobstructed view of the office and Justin.

Wonderful.

He snapped the emergency stop band around his waist and began his climb. The wooden rungs fit snugly into the palms of his hands as he moved. Most people at the gym would last less than two minutes, but Finn had been subjected to this beast long enough that he could manage nearly ten. As he moved, it was easy to fall into an unthinking state. His body screaming at him from the exertion, requiring all of his focus to keep from slipping. All he could do was stare straight ahead at the office and the occupants inside. Well, occupant—his gaze had pretty much landed on Justin and he hadn't been able to look away.

Finn watched as Justin pushed his dark-rimmed glasses up the bridge of his nose and pointed to something on the blueprints that were stretched over the office desk. He was wearing dress pants and a dress shirt again, and his cuffs were rolled up to the midpoint of his forearms.

Justin's actions were contained, no frantic waving of hands the way the contractor spoke. Finn knew from experience that Justin's words were well selected, each one absolutely necessary to get his point across, and nothing more. His body was lean, and Finn now knew what he felt like, even if he'd been left wanting more.

He knew what Justin tasted like as well.

"Jesus, he puts you on Jacobs Ladder?"

Finn started, losing his rhythm and nearly falling off the machine. "Shit."

Leo came up from behind him, arms crossed, and grinned. "I hate it. Why the hell would Eli make you use this?"

Finn's heart pounded even harder in his chest. "Endurance." He regained his footing and increased the pace.

"I guess that makes sense. Maybe I'll have to add it to my routine." Leo stepped closer and started to watch what he was doing. "Five minutes. That's not bad."

This is the part where you say something about your goals. About working your way up to doing this for twenty minutes straight. Maybe flirt a bit. "Thanks."

"I'm anxious for our date next week." Leo moved so he was now looking Finn directly in the eyes. "I want to hear all about your training routine. The things Eli has you doing. How you've progressed. I wish we could have gotten together sooner, but I'd already committed to going out with another guy. Don't want to be rude and bail."

"No. That's fine." Finn's hands were sweaty, making it more difficult to maintain his grasp on the rungs. But he wasn't about to break eye contact, not when Leo was paying such intense attention to him.

Leo paced beside the machine as he spoke. "I hope the Pear Tree is good for you? I've got to stick to my budget and all that crap."

"Sure. Yeah, that's good." For the first time since Finn had laid eyes on Leo, he wanted the other man to leave. It was getting incredibly hard to keep his pace up, and he was almost at his record. *I might finally break ten minutes. Shit, he's still talking.*

"You know what?" Leo snapped his fingers and grinned. "I'm free tomorrow night. Why don't we get together then instead?"

Finn stumbled, and rode the rung to the floor, triggering the emergency stop. "Tomorrow? We said next Friday." Friday was doable for him. It was *a week* away, which gave him time to work with Justin on what he was going to say.

Leo's smile dulled ever so slightly. "I know we did, but isn't tomorrow better? It's Saturday. We can talk about all sorts of things; maybe you can tell me how you made out today with your training?" Leo moved into Finn's personal space, close enough that Finn was worried he'd get sweat on him. "You can do tomorrow, right? I mean, this date is important, yeah?"

Oh God, it's not enough time. "Sure. Okay."

Leo traced his finger along the machine, so close to where Finn's arm was that he nearly touched it. "I'll see you there at five, then."

"But I—"

Leo blew him a kiss, turned, and left.

It took Finn a solid thirty seconds to make sense of what had just happened. Out of the blue, Leo had approached him and changed their date time. Had changed everything that he'd assumed was going to happen with a proverbial snap of his fingers. Finn wasn't ready for this. Not at all.

He was covered in sweat, his heart pounding out of his chest, and somehow needed to figure out how to get ready to go for an early supper. Tomorrow night. Not Friday like they'd planned.

Shit.

He looked up in time to see Justin staring at him from the office. Finn's chest tightened as blood rushed through him. He'd thought he had more time to prepare, more time to work on his introduction, to practice what he would say about his job so he wouldn't bore Leo to tears. God, he hadn't had a chance to work on what he'd gone over with Justin last night.

It was becoming difficult to pull air into his lungs. He had to force himself to breathe in through his nose, and out through his mouth so he wouldn't get too light-headed and pass out. Justin was still staring at him, and now took a step toward the door. Finn shook his head hard, stopping him in his tracks. *At least he listens to me.*

As much as he wanted to talk to Justin, to tell him what was going on, he had no right to disrupt his meeting. They weren't best buddies, even if Justin had shown him more kindness than nearly anyone else. Even if, despite everything that had happened between them last night, Finn really wanted Justin to ignore his request, come over, and help him figure out an action plan.

Instead, Finn moved over to the mat and began doing his jumping jacks.

Eli would find him shortly, and then he wouldn't be able to think about dates, freaking the fuck out, or anything else. He'd focus on the here and now, and only once he was done with his workout would he figure out how the hell he'd survive tomorrow night.

Justin wasn't easily distracted. Especially when he had to focus on a key project deliverable. Zack had been going back and forth with his contractor about the budget and the changes they'd like to make in the apartment. He and Zack had prepped beforehand, Zack wanting to take the lead in the meeting, with Justin offering his two cents when a decision had to be made.

That was why he'd been painfully aware of Finn climbing onto the torture machine Eli had mandated, why he'd known the second Finn looked at him, not to mention the instant Leo showed up and Finn freaked out. Justin hadn't been this hyperaware of another person since Grady had left Vancouver, and it was more than a little disconcerting.

Especially given how last night had ended.

"We can gut the kitchen next week. It's not big, but I have no clue what we'll find behind those walls. I need to know you have a contingency budget that I can draw on in case I need to."

Justin cleared his throat and glanced at the contractor. "We've allowed for a runover. The plumber has already identified several concerns, and we've taken those into account. Unless the electrical is worse than we're anticipating, then we should be covered."

When he looked back to Finn, he knew something had gone terribly wrong between him and Leo. Leo blew Finn a kiss, turned, and left Finn standing there appearing shell-shocked. Justin took a step toward the door, not that he knew what to do, but he wasn't about to abandon his new friend. But the second Finn shook his approach off, he forced his attention back to the matter at hand.

Because if everything went the way he and Zack were planning, his living arrangements were about to become entertaining.

Zack glanced over at Justin and frowned. "I don't want to start knocking down things until the custom cupboards are ready to ship. You've got to live in that mess, so I'd like to minimize the chaos as much as I can."

"I can manage. There's an excellent choice of takeout around here." Now that Justin had gotten a paycheck from Zack, that was something he could comfortably do. At least in the short term.

The contractor picked up his papers. "If I can start tearing walls down next week, then that gives us time to make sure any problems we find can be addressed before the cupboards arrive. I have a good supplier right now, and custom work has been coming reasonably fast."

Zack tapped his fingers against the desk. "I'm trusting you on this. Okay, let's move forward. Justin will then be able to start finding leads on clients for future apartment development. If we can get twenty percent rented, that will give us enough working capital to make the entire project profitable."

A few more details and a couple of handshakes and then the contractor was out the door. Justin sighed, relieved that the meeting was over. He turned to see that Finn was now in the ring with Eli. Eli was holding two giant pads for Finn to punch and kick.

Zack moved around behind him, the rustle of papers being rolled up and filed away filled the air. "How have things been going for you?" Zack sounded more like a CEO than a curious friend. "I know you've only been here a few weeks, but have you settled well upstairs? In the city?"

"I've finally managed to scrape the living organisms off the countertops in the apartment. I'll be almost sorry to see them go." Justin tore his gaze away from Finn to look at Zack. "Almost."

"Nolan said Finn came up to help run cables?"

Rogers Cable had arrived, and he now had high-speed internet. Justin might have even given a fist pump once the installers left. "He did. I can now binge-watch Netflix to my heart's content."

"The two of you seem to have hit it off."

Justin crossed his arms, preparing for what was clearly an interrogation. "I'm helping him with a little problem he has. That's all."

"Really?" Zack snorted. "Nolan was shocked to have seen the two of you together at the speed dating event. It's my understanding Finn doesn't really talk to many people."

"And I'm not exactly the warm fuzzy type."

"I didn't mean that."

"Yes, you did." He'd been told how much of a cold bastard he could be over the years. "I promise, I'm not abusing any of your patrons."

"You don't like to make it easy for people to like you, do you?"

"Being liked was never one of my goals. You can't be everyone's friend and have your business be number one." That was something he'd firmly believed working for Theo Barnes—still did if he was being honest with himself. "It's why I had to leave Vancouver in the first place."

"I used to work with a lot of people like you at Compass Technologies. Hell, I used to be like you."

Justin had heard all about Zack Anderson, asshole and CTO of Compass, from Grady and Max over supper the other night. He hadn't quite been able to reconcile what he'd heard about Zack and the man he saw on a nearly daily basis here at Ringside. "What changed?"

"Nolan." Simply saying his partner's name made Zack's entire demeanor soften. "He showed up, and I realized that there was a different way of doing things. It took me a while to accept that I could have it all: a solid relationship, kindness, a successful business. I just had to change my perspective on life."

"As easy as that." Except, it was nothing but. The fortune might favor the brave, but it also tended to reward the aggressive, uncaring manipulator as well. It was a fine line that Justin often found himself on the wrong side of.

The farther away he'd removed himself from his past, the less he knew what to do with himself in the future. All he had were his instincts and his words.

And quite a challenging project in Finn.

After he'd left Finn's place last night, Justin had decided to take a step back from what had happened and examine his actions. Why he'd allowed himself to get caught up in the moment was beyond him, an anomaly of his normally reserved self. Finn had overwhelmed his sensibilities with his shy smiles and intense gazes. Justin hadn't been on the receiving end of that sort of attention before.

It had been flattering, and unexpectedly arousing.

It couldn't happen again.

Finn wanted Leo. He'd been quite clear in his request and hadn't wavered in any of the conversations they'd had. It wasn't his fault Justin had let things go too far, had allowed himself to get taken in. Nor was it Finn's fault that Justin had been able to see himself in the role of *better than Leo*.

He was here to help Finn win Leo over. Nothing more.

Zack cleared his throat. "I think his time with Eli is almost up. If you wanted to go over and say hello."

Jesus, the last thing Justin needed was for others to start meddling in his personal life. "I see that."

"Are you going to talk to him?"

"I have to. We've made eye contact."

"Right. It would be rude to ignore him now."

Justin somehow managed to keep his sigh inside. "Say hello to Nolan for me." Knowing Zack wouldn't give up until he spoke to Finn, Justin left the office as Finn headed back toward the locker room.

Sweat covered his body, making his black hair darker than normal, slick and stuck to his forehead. Somehow, his crystal-blue eyes appeared to sparkle. "You look quite disgusting."

Finn's smiled brightened the room. "Eli's an asshole."

"I've heard that from more than one person." Justin knew he should let Finn go and have a shower, but he couldn't quite get himself to move out of the way. "I saw you speaking to Leo earlier. I was concerned. You appeared upset."

And as quickly as Finn's relaxation was there, in a flash it was gone. "I need to talk to you about that. Ah . . . something's changed."

"That sounds ominous." Justin swallowed past an unexpected tightening of his throat. *Did Leo break things off before they'd begun?* "Why don't you come up to my apartment once you've cleaned up and we can talk about it?"

"Yeah, thanks." Finn wiped a hand down his face, taking sweat with it. "Give me twenty minutes and I'll be right there."

Ignoring the fleeting image of Finn naked in a shower, Justin nodded. "Of course. The door will be unlocked, just come right in."

He turned and made a direct line for the back stairs, his words rolling through his head like a mantra.

You're only here to help. He's not yours.

═ CHAPTER ═
TWELVE

Finn knocked on Justin's door out of habit before opening it. The kitchen was far cleaner and more organized than it had been on his previous visit. The coffee maker was tucked away in the corner, next to a toaster, which was a new addition. There was a dish rack that had a single plate and cup turned upside-down and dry.

They painted a strangely lonely picture.

"Justin?" He kicked off his shoes and dropped his gym bag on the floor by the door.

"I'll be out in a moment."

Another new piece of equipment was the watercooler off to the side of the fridge. Presumably, that meant the plumber hadn't quite addressed all the problems yet. At least the place no longer smelled of dead . . . something. He'd been concerned for Justin's health.

"Mind if I get a drink?"

"There are a few glasses in the cupboard by the fridge." A bang of a small door echoed through the apartment.

Still dehydrated from working out, Finn didn't hesitate to find and fill a glass. It wasn't until he'd filled it a second time that Justin strode out from the bedroom. "Sorry about that. Given how little I have here, you'd think I'd be able to find items when I go hunting for them."

Finn's gaze locked onto Justin's body. Gone was the dress shirt he'd been wearing before, replaced by a tight-fitting black Ringside Gym shirt. If Finn had thought Justin was an attractive man in the dress shirts he always wore, then seeing him dressed in a skin-tight T-shirt blew that estimation out of the water. "That's . . . different."

Justin looked down at the shirt and shrugged. "I just spilled coffee all over myself. I don't plan on going anywhere else today, so I figured I'd go casual while my shirt soaks. I *do* know how to relax." The way he said that suggested it was a comment he'd had to say frequently about himself.

"Never figured you didn't."

Justin's lips pressed into a tight line, as he tugged on the hem of his shirt. "I didn't have anything else clean. I need to do my laundry today."

"You look fine. Great even." Finn face heated. "Sorry."

"No reason to be." And in a snap, Justin was back to his earlier demeanor. "Why don't you tell me about your problem? From the look of things downstairs, Leo said something that sent you into a panic."

The brief mental respite Finn had been enjoying vanished. "He moved the date up."

"To when?"

"Tomorrow night. I'm not ready for that." There was a real possibility that he'd never be ready for his date with Leo. But tomorrow night? The few lessons he'd had with Justin had already evaporated from his mind.

Justin braced his hands on his hips. "That could be a problem."

"You think? It's going to be a fucking disaster." Finn's legs shook, and he sat down on the small couch that now took up a portion of Justin's living room. "The thought of it makes me sick. I don't know what to do."

"What we're going to do is practice a few things tonight. We'll have a trial conversation, work out possible scenarios and topics. You'll do fine."

Finn let out a whimper. *So manly.*

"I'm serious." Justin crossed the room and sat down on the couch beside him. "You proved last night that when you're relaxed, you handle yourself just fine. Maybe that's what we should be focusing on instead. Teaching you how to relax."

"I do yoga."

"You clearly need to do more."

"What I *need* is for you to go on the date with me and answer all of his questions on my behalf. That would be amazing. I'll whisper what I want to say, and then you can make me sound eloquent." That would make all of his problems go away. With Justin as his mouth piece, he'd no doubt end up with Leo as his boyfriend.

Wait a minute . . .

Finn turned to Justin, inadvertently pressing his thigh fully against Justin's. "I have an idea."

"I realize we don't know each other all that well, but even I can tell that I'm not going to like your idea." Justin's gaze dropped to where their bodies touched, but he didn't move away.

"I have a friend who's into a bunch of security stuff. He's an investigator, but also works as hired security for events and stuff. He has an ear piece for communication with people in the security office. I can see if I can borrow some of his equipment. You can listen in on the date and help me out with things to say if I get stuck." Shit, why hadn't he thought of this earlier? It would have saved him hours of worry.

Justin cocked his head to the side. "That's by far the creepiest thing I've ever heard."

"No, it's not. I'll still be the one on the date and doing the talking. You'll just be my unseen moral support."

"It's dangerously close to stalking." Justin shifted away from him then, his face screwed up into a grimace. "I don't want to be witness to your private moment."

"If you don't, there won't be much of a private moment at all. I know me: I'll panic and leave before appetizers are done." If he made it that far at all.

Justin sighed. "Have you ever considered the idea that if you're this nervous around Leo, then he might not be the man for you?"

Finn blinked. "No. He's exactly my type."

"How do you know? You've barely spoken to him."

Devan had asked him that question once before, so it was something he'd thought long and hard about. "He's the picture of the man I used to fantasize about when I was a teen. The blond hair and his smiles. The way he makes a room brighter just from walking into it. Everyone is drawn to him because he's so easygoing. And when he looks at me, I feel special. I don't think I've ever been with anyone that's made me feel like that."

Justin didn't break eye contact as Finn spoke, which made Finn's heart beat a bit faster. That was one thing Justin and Leo had in common.

Justin then nodded, but his gaze shifted to the floor. "I had someone like that in my life. I became quite infatuated after years of spending days alongside him."

Finn hadn't really considered who Justin would have in his life. That he'd had a life before he'd showed up at the gym two weeks ago. "Who was it?"

"Grady."

"Grady Barnes from downstairs?"

"The very one."

"But . . . he's with Max."

If Finn hadn't been staring directly at Justin, he wouldn't have noticed the small change in his demeanor. It wasn't that he was angry or annoyed at what was clearly a bad situation for him, but rather, sad. "He is. And far happier than I would ever have made him."

Sure, Finn might not know Justin well, but he was a smart, attractive man. Finn couldn't understand why Grady, or anyone else for that matter, wouldn't be all over him. "What happened?"

"Familiarity breeds contempt." When Finn didn't say anything, Justin turned his head to look him in the eye. "I worked for Grady's father. I was essentially hired to keep Grady in line, which for the record was not an easy task. When you've spent ten years of your life keeping tabs on another person, it stands to reason that the object of your meddling wouldn't want to get involved in a relationship."

"You were only doing what you were told to do. I can't imagine he'd hate you for doing your job."

"Perhaps if I hadn't performed my job with such enthusiasm, that would be the case." Justin chuckled. "Once he and Max got together, I realized that any feelings I'd developed for Grady were wrong. I'd known him when he was a teen and watched him grow into a man. I guess that makes me a creep."

Finn shook his head. "You're not creepy. Grady was lucky to have you around."

"I'm not so sure. Thankfully, we do appear to still have a friendship of sorts. I'm grateful for that."

It was strange to see Justin, a man who seemed to have had an impenetrable suit of armor around him, struggling with an invisible wound. "I'm grateful as well."

"For what?"

"That whatever happened in your past brought you here. While I'm aware that things between me and Leo might not work out, I'm happy to have gotten a new friend out of this."

Instead of the smile Finn had hoped to get, Justin rubbed his hands on his legs before standing abruptly. "Go get your equipment from your friend. Let's do this so you can get your man."

Relief was tinged with a bit of embarrassment as Finn stood as well. "Thanks, man. I don't think I can do this without you." He turned around the apartment, trying to find some way of repaying Justin for his kindness. "How about I come back with my tools and I fix . . . something. What's your contractor doing?"

"You don't have to—"

"I absolutely do. I need to repay you for what you're doing. And I'll no doubt need a distraction after the date. So, what can I tear apart?"

Justin didn't move at first, but then slowly shook his head, a small smile appearing. "I have the contractor coming to start on the kitchen next week. I don't know, maybe we can work on the walls here in the living room."

"Deal. The date is tomorrow, so how about I come over Sunday to help you out?"

Justin appeared to mull that over before shrugging. "Why not. I don't have plans." That note of sadness was back again.

The longer Finn spent with him, the more he realized how lonely Justin was. Given all Justin was trying to do for him, what he was asking Justin to do tomorrow night, this was the very least that he could do. It wasn't exactly a hardship, being with him, so Finn was getting the better end on both accounts.

"Okay, the equipment. I can stop by here an hour before my date. I'll show you how the equipment works, and I'll even bring you supper." He really had enjoyed cooking for Justin the other night.

"Sounds good."

It was obvious from the way Justin spoke that he was expecting Finn to leave now. It was what Finn had intended to do, if he was being honest with himself. He'd come and gotten what he'd hoped he would, so there wasn't any reason to stay.

Except...

He was using Justin and not giving him much in return. Sure, he'd agreed to do a little home improvement for him, but that didn't quite seem on par with what Justin was doing for him. Finn knew he was going to owe Justin a long time if things worked out between him and Leo. "Say, are you doing anything tonight?"

His question had clearly caught Justin off guard. "No."

"It's just, I don't think I can actually get any more work done, especially with tomorrow night now a thing. I was wondering, ah, maybe you might want to go out tonight. I mean just as friends. To do something. Not like a date. I don't think I could handle two dates in a week."

For the first time since he'd met Justin, Finn saw the other man blush. "I wouldn't know where to go."

His rush of excitement was a bit unexpected, but Finn took it as a good thing. "Well, you said you know Grady. Doesn't his boyfriend own a club? At least, I thought that's what I'd heard someone say."

"Frantic. It's a dance bar—very loud from the one time I was there."

Not his ideal evening out, but doing something out of the ordinary would be good for a change. "Sure. I like to dance."

Justin cocked an eyebrow. "That's... I can't picture that at all."

"What? You think techies don't have rhythm?"

"Not in my experience."

The dark cloud that had descended on them moments earlier lifted. Finn wasn't sure what was coming over him, but he started swaying his hips to an invisible beat. "Dude, what do you think we do when we're waiting for servers to reboot or software patches to load? We dance."

Justin's face morphed from disbelief to amusement as Finn got into his solo dance. Turning around, he gave his ass a little shake and suddenly, Justin was laughing. "Dear God, stop."

"Now that's a sound I didn't think I'd hear." Finn turned back around and moved a bit closer to Justin. "You have a great laugh, and you should use it more."

Justin pushed his glasses up the bridge of his nose. "I haven't had much reason to laugh in recent months."

"Well, I'm going to help you change that. I have to go home for a bit, but I'll come back. We'll get something to eat, then go over. If nothing else, you can look forward to laughing at my wicked moves."

"Actually"—Justin shrugged in a way that was far cuter than it should have been—"they have excellent cheeseburgers there."

Finn's stomach growled at the thought. "Yes. That's perfect." It *was* perfect, and that rarely happened in his life. "I'll be back at six, and then we can head over for that cheeseburger."

"Sure. If you're determined to do this."

"I am."

"Then I guess I'll have to change my shirt after all."

Finn walked over to him, stopping once their shoulders were nearly touching. "You don't have to. It looks pretty good on you."

Without waiting to see Justin's reaction, Finn grabbed his bag and fled.

CHAPTER THIRTEEN

I f someone had told Justin a few months ago that he'd be excited at the prospect of having a cheeseburger with a man he barely knew, at a club that was testosterone filled and populated with sweaty, horny men, he would never have believed it. These weren't his people, this wasn't his scene, and this certainly wasn't the music he enjoyed.

And yet, here he sat at a table, dipping his French fries into his mayo and smiling at the man sitting across from him. Apparently, good company could make up for a multitude of other sins.

Finn's head had pretty much been on a pivot since their arrival forty minutes previous. It was still too early for dancing, and most of the people here were either playing pool, eating, or sharing a drink. The music playing over the speakers was loud, but Justin and Finn had been able to talk with little effort.

"I had no idea this place was this much fun." Finn's voice reached him easily in between songs. "Not that I'd come here on my own, but this is great."

"A gay bar would be an ideal location for you to go alone. You could practice talking to strangers." It would be perfect if for no other reason than it might get Finn thinking about someone—anyone—other than Leo. "I'll make sure to pass along your approval to Max."

Justin had seen Max behind the bar when they'd first arrived, but he'd managed to move away before he was recognized. While he and Max had come to a sort of truce since his arrival to Toronto, he didn't want to put himself in line for the teasing that was sure to come when Max realized Justin was here with a man.

Even if it wasn't a date.

Neither he nor Finn would ever be ready for that.

Finn took another big bite from his burger, and Justin couldn't help but watch as his tongue darted out to lick a dollop of ketchup from the corner of his mouth. This was something new for Justin, this sudden infatuation with every little move another person was making. It was embarrassing, or would be if Finn ever found out what he was doing. At least that wouldn't happen. Justin imagined Finn only had room for one infatuation at a time.

Swallowing some of his beer, Justin pushed away the thoughts that threatened to take him down a path that wouldn't be helpful for either of them. "We should talk about tomorrow night."

He'd half expected Finn to jump at the chance, but he looked more than a little disappointed at the suggestion. "You know, if it's okay with you, I'd rather not."

Justin gave his head a shake as he fingered the bottom of his beer mug. "Whatever you'd like."

"What I'd like is to finish this amazing burger. Eli's going to kill me for eating something this delicious, because there's no way it's good for me. Then I'll end up putting on weight that isn't lean muscle, and he'll make me do extra minutes on Jacobs Ladder."

The music changed songs, this time to one with a punishingly loud bassline, forcing Justin to nod his agreement. Finn's eyes continued to dart around the bar as they ate. Justin couldn't help but follow his gaze, trying to learn a bit more about the man sitting across from him; what music he would bob his head to, what things in the bar would catch his attention. *Who* would catch his attention.

That was the strangest part of all. Finn didn't appear to be staring at any one person. Even as the dance floor began to fill, he seemed interested in objects, the laughter that would filter through the blasting music, or large groups socializing.

Justin shifted his attention to the bar where Max still stood. He was a tall man, with a ready smile and a deep chuckle. Justin hadn't wanted to, but from their initial meeting in the alley behind this very club, he had grudgingly respected Max. When Justin had offered him a bribe, Max had declined. When Justin had tried to get Max away from Grady, he'd refused to go. Justin had quickly realized, even as he'd been certain that their engagement was fake, that there was something far deeper going on between Max and Grady.

Which had meant that Justin would be cast aside. His usefulness had been over.

God, he was tired of being cast aside.

The *crack* of pool balls smacking against one another seemed to catch Finn's attention. There was a small area setup behind where they were sitting: two pool tables and several lounge chairs tucked into the corner of the club. Finn turned to stare at them, then back to Justin with a grin. "Do you happen to play?"

"Learned when I was ten." It had been one of the few things Justin had done with his father on a semiregular basis. Every Sunday as soon as they got home from church, Justin had been expected to rack the balls on the table in their basement, and he and his father would play a game. Not that Justin ever won, but he'd appreciated the small parcel of time his father had given him.

"I suck at it, but love to play." Finn set his napkin down on the now-empty plate. "Think we can win a table?"

Justin looked over, quickly evaluating the skills of the men currently playing. "Absolutely."

Finn got to his feet and strangely, held out his hand for Justin to take. "Come on, then."

Justin shouldn't have touched Finn, shouldn't have slipped his hand into the open waiting palm. But logic and reasoning seemed to have abandoned him these days, and he did exactly that. The warmth from Finn's large hand wrapping around his sent a shiver through him. This was stupid and horrible and so completely out of character, he hardly recognized himself.

Finn led him to the pool tables. "Hey, guys. Can we get in on a game?"

One of the men playing shrugged. "He's kicking my ass. Go for it." And he laid his cue down. "I'm going to hit the bar."

The remaining man looked up and smiled. Ah, that was an expression Justin had seen more than once: cockiness. "Sure. One of you beat me, and the table's yours."

Finn dropped Justin's hand and turned to him. "I can try, but it takes me a while to warm up."

"No need. I've got this." Justin had ignored Finn's earlier request and changed back into a dress shirt before coming out tonight.

Strangely, he always felt more comfortable like this than in anything the least bit casual. He undid the buttons of his cuffs and rolled his shirt sleeves halfway up his arms, before stepping to the table. "Flip for break?"

"Okay." The man pulled a quarter from his pocket. "Heads."

The coin landed on heads, and Justin couldn't help but smile. While winning the break would have been beneficial, it was far from necessary. "Would you like me to rack?"

"Go for it." The man chalked his cue off to the side, but Justin was aware of him watching his every move.

This was like being back in the office. People trying to gauge one another without being obvious about it. It was one of the reasons his father had insisted on teaching him the game in the first place. Justin made sure to take his time putting the balls in the rack. Nothing fancy. He set them up, pulled the rack away, and grabbed a cue of his own. "All set."

The man sunk two balls off the break, one low and one high. It wasn't a great leave, but he managed to sink the two ball, before missing on the four. "You're up."

Justin took a moment to evaluate the various shots open to him. He settled on a shot that shouldn't scare the man away, but would show his skill. "Twelve, cross side." Without much preamble, he lined up and sunk the shot.

The man straightened. "Nice."

"Thank you. Ten, left corner." Another lineup, another ball sunk.

Justin put the nine and fifteen down as quickly and the man rested his cue against the wall. "Given the shots you just made and what's left on the table, I know you can run this. I concede. Have fun, guys."

Finn clapped when the man walked away. "That was impressive. Congratulations."

He shouldn't have felt a tingle of pride at Finn's praise, but he did. He also couldn't help but feel a tiny bit disappointed. He'd wanted to show off a bit, show Finn that he was good at something other than preparing speeches to help him win a man who wasn't worthy of his time. Justin cleared his throat. "Why don't you rack them and we can play a game?"

"Don't worry about kicking my ass. I'm going to enjoy watching you play even if I lose horribly. You said you were ten when you learned?"

"My father taught me. Every week for an hour. Over time I got reasonably good at it."

Finn laughed, making his crystal-blue eyes sparkle. "I know a shark when I see one. All you're missing is the fin."

I've got my Finn right here. "Fair enough. I'll let you break."

They played several games over the course of a half hour. Finn wasn't nearly as bad as he'd tried to let on. And while Justin was the better of the two of them, he'd made a few basic mistakes due to his split attention. Because every time Finn would lean over the table to make a shot, Justin had to look long and hard at the very perfect ass in front of him, and it took a while to clear his head.

Justin was becoming infatuated with Finn. That had only happened once before in his life, and Justin had to believe Grady still held some resentment toward him for it. He needed to keep his distance, and let Finn have his moment with Leo. That was what Finn wanted and what Justin had agreed to. Everything else was little more than a distraction.

But that ass . . .

His focus on Finn was the reason he didn't notice Grady was beside him until it was too late. Grady leaned in with a smile. "I can't believe you're here."

"I didn't know you were here either." He should have suspected Grady would be wherever Max was, but it hadn't crossed his mind.

Finn shifted to reach a ball far across the table, shifting his hips. Justin cleared his throat and forced his eyes away. "I'm here with Finn. We're working on . . . a project."

A wide grin split Grady's face. "Oh, is that what we're calling it these days?"

It wasn't his place to let anyone else know what Finn's plan was. So, he kept his mouth shut and took Grady's teasing. "Finn, you remember Grady Barnes?"

Finn looked up from his shot. He had no poker face: his expression morphed from shock and awe, to an embarrassed smile. "Hey."

"Hey yourself. I hope this jerk isn't taking advantage of you. He can be quite the pool shark when he wants to be."

The comment was obviously meant to be teasing, but it stung nonetheless. "You know me, always pulling strings behind the curtain."

Finn's smile slipped. "He's . . . ah, well . . . helping me. I mean, my game."

Grady was clearly oblivious to Finn's discomfort. He took the cue from Justin, holding it out of reach. "Justin as a helper? Yeah, that's different." He smiled at Justin. "Though I'm glad it's not you meddling or something. There's nothing worse than when you'd get onto the warpath and get determined to set matters right."

Finn turned fully around, resting his cue against the table. He said nothing, but his body was shaking and his face had gone pale. Justin took a step toward him, but Grady stopped him by putting his arm across Justin's shoulders. "Hey, remember that time you got mad at me when I lost a pool game at Father's club? God, I thought you were such a bully." He moved them both over to Finn and draped an arm over Finn's shoulders. Grady looked between them with a grin. "I was an absolute brat back then."

Finn no longer appeared to be paying attention to Grady. His eyes had widened, and his body had tensed, but he didn't make a move. For some reason, he looked petrified.

"Grady, I need you to let go." Justin couldn't take his eyes from Finn. There was something else going on here, something that wasn't going to end well if Justin didn't act now.

"Oh come on—I'm just talking." Grady gave Finn a little shake, but did let him go. "So, tell me about yourself, Finn. You're quite the animal in the ring."

Finn's mouth opened, but nothing came out.

Justin tried to move away from Grady, but he didn't let go. "Grady, can you please—"

"I don't really talk to Eli, but when I see him, he's always singing your praises. Do you like fighting? You could probably go pro. Think you'd enjoy being in the ring full-time?"

Before Justin registered what had happened, Finn was pressed up against the wall, his body shaking and his breathing coming out in harsh gasps.

Justin threw off Grady's arm and crossed over to stand close to Finn. "Are you okay?"

Finn shook his head without making eye contact. Justin wanted to do something, but there was a crowd starting to form and the last thing Finn would want was to become the center of a spectacle. "Can we have some room here?"

In that brief moment as Justin turned to the crowd, Grady moved next to Finn. "Dude, are you okay?"

One second, Grady was touching Finn's shoulder, and in the next he was flying to the floor as Finn shoved him away, hard. Grady tripped over the pool cue that had been leaning against the table, sending him crashing to the floor. Grady's head bounced off the leg of a bystander, drawing everyone's attention.

"Get out of my way." Max pushed through the small crowd that had formed around them. "What the fuck is going on in my club?"

Of course Max would have seen Grady get hurt and race over. Justin moved beside Finn, knowing he had precious little time to de-escalate the situation before things went from bad to worse. "He's having a panic attack."

Finn was sweating and his eyes were wide. "I just . . . I need to leave."

Max knelt down to help Grady back up, but thankfully neither of them came any closer. Justin chanced a look at Max, giving him a small nod before turning his full attention back to Finn. "He was asking you too many questions and you got overwhelmed. That's fine. He shouldn't have touched you, but he's handsy that way."

Grady got back to his feet. "I'm not *handsy*. More like touchy-feely."

Max growled. "Shut up."

It took a few minutes, but slowly the panic in Finn's eyes cleared, only to be replaced with embarrassment. "I'm sorry. So sorry." He stepped away from the wall, his face flushed. "I'm heading home."

"I'll come with you." Justin held the cue out for Max to take. "Sorry for the disruption. Grady . . . we should probably talk. Later."

"Yup." Grady rubbed his side. "I'll give you a call."

Justin placed his hand on the center of Finn's back and navigated him toward the door. "Let's get you home."

Finn's body continued to shake until they got back to his condo. Justin didn't say a word, didn't make any obvious moves to try to comfort him, but neither did he break physical contact with him during the entire trip. It wasn't until they stepped inside his condo that Finn felt the tension bleed from his muscles. He made it over to the couch before the energy that had gotten him this far finally dissipated. King trotted over, jumped up, and settled tight against his thigh.

"Fuck." Finn let his head fall into his hands. "I'm so sorry."

"For making Grady realize he was being an ass? Don't be. He's already texted me twice apologizing for what he did." Justin sat down beside him and gave his knee a squeeze. "He means well. Our history is . . . complicated."

"I gathered."

"I get the impression that you have some complications of your own."

"Yeah."

Justin mirrored his pose, their legs side by side, knees touching. "Have you talked to anyone about being bullied?"

"I'm thirty-two years old. It's a bit late for that."

"It's impacting your daily life. Your ability to talk to others. Seeing a counselor could help you get a handle on your history, emotions, and dealing with situations like that."

No, it would make him feel miserable, and he'd still have to live with the memories of what had happened to him all those years ago. "Maybe."

What he wanted . . . no, needed, was to get ready for his date with Leo tomorrow night. A good night's sleep would help him put matters into perspective. "I'm tired."

"I'll let you get some rest, then." But Justin didn't move.

Strangely, Finn didn't want him to leave. He couldn't explain why, but the world seemed less heavy, less overwhelming when Justin was around. "Your place sucks."

"It's fine. I have a mattress now. No box spring, but that's on my list."

"Stay here." When Justin pulled back, Finn looked up and realized how his words sounded. "I mean, you can sleep on the couch.

It's pretty late and this thing is really comfy. I've slept here a lot. In the morning, we can get something to eat and I can grab the equipment."

Justin cocked his head, his mouth opening and closing, but no words emerging. Finn reached out and slid his hand along Justin's thigh, giving it a gentle squeeze. "You'd be doing me a favor."

Justin nodded slowly, as he ran his tongue across his bottom lip. "Very well."

"I'll get you some blankets and a pillow." He stood and instantly missed Justin's warmth.

When he got back, Justin was standing once again, browsing through his books. King had jumped from the couch and was now sitting beside Justin, looking up at him. Justin touched the edge of the bookshelf. "I didn't thank you for earlier."

The blankets made a soft *whoosh* at they landed on the couch cushions. "For what?"

"I've ... I'm not exactly the sort of man who inspires friendship in others. I've always been seen as an obstacle to get around so they can achieve their goal. Normally, they're correct. Tonight ... It's nice to be seen. Not simply as a *thing*, but as a person. A friend. Thank you for wanting me to stay tonight. As a friend." He looked away, back toward the books. "You better get some sleep. You're going to need your rest for tomorrow."

"You too." With his heart pounding, Finn swallowed hard. "Good night."

"Good night."

With emotions he couldn't name swirling inside him, Finn went to his bedroom and quietly closed the door.

CHAPTER FOURTEEN

The smell of coffee and bacon was what eventually brought Justin back to the land of the living. He cracked open his eyes only to come face-to-face with a small canine nose sniffing him from the edge of the couch.

Justin gave King's head a scratch. "He's cooking."

King cocked his head to the side, as though he were running Justin's words through an interpretation algorithm.

"I bet he has a treat for you."

King cocked his head to the other side, before making a soft *ruff* noise and trotting to the kitchen.

Justin stretched out on the couch, loosening his muscles as he closed his eyes again. It had taken him a long time to go to sleep after Finn had disappeared into his room. The couch was comfortable enough, but his thoughts hadn't been. He'd lain there, eyes glued to a spot on the ceiling, thinking about what had happened at Frantic. Yes, Grady had crossed a line. Yes, Finn had overreacted, and somehow Max hadn't. All of those things were facts and shouldn't have bothered him. Didn't in fact.

No, what had prevented sleep from taking him was that, somehow, a man who suffered from social anxiety had chosen him as a confidant. Justin, a man who had no close friends growing up, and had very few as an adult. Finn, who only seemed to be able to talk to people over the phone, was comfortable conversing with him in person and had been since day one. And for the life of him, he didn't know how to feel about it.

The sound of a mug being placed on the coffee table beside him did the last bit of work to pull him from sleep. Finn had quickly disappeared, but the glorious mug of steaming coffee was there waiting when Justin opened his eyes again. He took the mug in his hand as he sat up. "You're a prince."

"And good morning to you. Sleep okay?" Finn's voice came from the kitchen.

Justin wasn't quite ready to face him, so he stayed put. "The couch was as comfortable as advertised." The first sip of coffee made his world slow to the point of nothing else existing beyond the black liquid before him. The second had him melting. "You should be a barista."

"I was for a while. I didn't last very long."

Justin got up and wandered over to the kitchen. Again, he was struck by how natural Finn looked preparing food. "Scratch that. I'm going back to my original assertion that you should be a chef."

Finn smiled and shook his head. "How about I just cook for you?"

"Works for me."

Finn walked over to where King sat and filled his bowl with dog food, only to place a strip of bacon on top of it. "Eat it slow."

King swallowed it in two bites, before devouring the rest of his food, and padding off to his dog bed in the corner.

Justin watched Finn cook a few moments longer before asking the inevitable. "How are you feeling this morning?"

When Finn's gaze met his, Justin momentarily stopped breathing. There was such gratitude there, he couldn't believe it was directed at him. Finn's smile made his eyes sparkle. "Much better. Thanks."

"That's good." Justin's insides were doing a squirmy dance, but he did his best to ignore it. "When do you get the equipment from your friend?"

"I got it already." Finn placed a plate with more food than Justin could possibly eat in front of him. "I had to get eggs, so I ducked over to Tyrell's place and got what I needed. Eat up."

While Justin did exactly that, Finn brought over a black case and opened it up on the counter beside them. "It's an Invisity Ear Prompter. It's got a great range, so I should be able to hear you no problem from the restaurant. You don't even have to leave your apartment. Tyrell said he's used it in a stadium before and had no issues, so our little project should work fine."

And in a flash, Justin's good mood bled away. When he'd agreed to help Finn with his date, Justin hadn't realized how entangled his emotions would be. How hard it would be to help him build a relationship with Leo. Or anyone else.

Justin wanted Finn for himself.

He cleared his throat and did his best to squash those complicated feelings. "How will I hear what's being said?"

Finn didn't quite meet his gaze as he shuffled the equipment. "I'll have a microphone as well. It should be strong enough to pick up both what I'm saying and what Leo's saying. Everything should go smoothly."

"I hope so." The food no longer held its amazing taste. Justin pushed the eggs around before finally picking up a piece of bacon and shoving it all into his mouth. This was ridiculous. When he'd started out with wanting to help Finn, he'd never anticipated that spying would be a part of it; though, he was willing to do it, especially if it would make Finn happy. And despite everything else, that was Justin's main and only goal.

He played with the eggs on his plate a moment longer before taking a bite. "We still need to practice."

Finn looked up and blinked. "We do?"

"Of course, we do. I need you to show me how all this works. Unlike yourself, I'm not technically inclined. We also need to make sure you're used to hearing me talking in your ear. You don't want to appear to be hesitating too much."

"Yeah, that makes sense." Finn straightened. "Thanks."

"You're welcome. Here's what we're going to do. I'm going to finish eating my breakfast, then I'm going to head home to get cleaned up. Your date is at five, right?"

"Yup."

"Come over at three and we'll rehearse. By six, I suspect things will be going well enough that you won't even need this and I'll be able to get back to working on scum removal in my apartment." Justin stuck out his hand and waited for Finn to take it. "Deal?"

Finn slipped his hand into Justin's. "Deal."

Justin didn't hold his hand long, knowing the longer they touched, the harder it would be for him to keep a level head.

"Fantastic. Now, I need to eat what I can, and possibly ask for a doggy bag. While Zack pays me well, I have so many things I need to buy to set-up my life in Toronto, I don't have extra for bacon. Or eggs. Or bread."

Finn chuckled. "I can put together a care package for you, if you want."

"Chips. I would kill for potato chips." Justin had few vices in life, but those were one of them.

"Dude, given everything that you're doing for me, I'll buy you stock in Lay's if that's what you want." Finn was on the move once more, gathering food to put into containers.

"Have you given any thought about what you're going to wear tonight?"

Finn shrugged. "I've been obsessing over that almost as much as I've been worrying about what I plan to say."

"I'd suggest the outfit you wore to the speed dating event." Justin took a bit of toast, and moaned at the richness of the real butter that had become trapped in the crevices of the bread. "You looked fantastic."

Finn's blush was cute. "Thanks. Yeah, I can do that."

"Good." While Justin had perfect recollection of what Finn had on that night, he suspected Leo wouldn't have noticed if Finn had been naked. "And make sure you put on that cologne you had on last night. That works well on you."

It was strange, but plying Finn with compliments was quickly becoming one of Justin's favorite things to do. Clearly, Finn hadn't gotten nearly enough of those over the years, which made no sense to Justin whatsoever. Finn was a handsome man, kind and intelligent. Just because he had a hard time conversing in social situations, didn't mean he should be any less appealing to others. Hell, if Leo couldn't see the gift he was being offered, Justin fully intended to smash him over the head with something, until he did.

Finn deserved to be happy.

Justin was going to make sure that would happen.

It didn't take long for Justin to eat his fill, and for Finn to pack up the leftovers for him. Justin held up the containers. "I'll bring this back to you tomorrow."

"No rush. I know where you live."

Justin collected his things, while Finn trailed along behind him. King raced to the door when he realized Justin was leaving, barking several times. The situation was comforting rather than off-putting. The dog, having Finn's body that close—it felt intimate, as though they'd done this dozens of times instead of just once.

He cleared his throat. "I'll leave my door open for you. Just walk in when you get there."

Finn leaned a hand against the wall, opening his body up to Justin. "I will. Though you probably should keep your door locked. That can be a rough neighborhood."

"No one even knows there's anyone up there. I'll be fine." *Kiss him!* "I'll see you later."

Finn swayed a bit closer, but not enough for Justin to take advantage. "Yup."

Before he acted on any foolish impulses, Justin turned and left.

The moment Justin walked into Ringside to access the stairway to the apartments, he realized something was going on. A crowd had formed around the ring, and the air was full of shouts and cheers as two combatants were going at it in the ring.

As hard as he tried, Justin didn't enjoy boxing. The thought of two people beating the ever-living shit out of one another was as far from his version of entertainment as he could imagine. Others clearly didn't share his view.

It was hard to get a sense of who was in the ring, as both opponents had head protectors on. He was about to continue on, when a shout caught his attention.

"Kick his ass, Leo!"

Justin drew to a stop, pivoted, and made his way to the back of the crowd. While Finn was home, no doubt practicing what he wanted to say, the object of his desire was currently landing a series of punches on his opponent.

Now that he knew who it was, Justin couldn't believe he hadn't been able to tell from the moment he walked in. Leo's swagger was easily recognizable, as was his more-than-ripped physique. While Finn's muscles seemed to compliment his body, Leo's appeared little more than globs of meat slapped onto a frame. They bulged in ways that didn't look normal, and Justin swore his legs were too small to carry around his massive torso.

Whoever was in the ring with Leo certainly wasn't any match. Leo landed punch after punch, and his challenger stumbled backward. The bell rang, but Leo took one final swing, connecting with the other man's chin. Justin could only watch in horror as the man dropped like a dead weight to the canvas.

Part of the crowd exploded in cheers, but several people booed. Justin tapped the shoulder of a young woman standing beside him. "Was he allowed to do that?"

"No. Leo's a fucking dirty fighter. Totally a late hit."

Someone must have gotten Zack, because he came racing from the office. "What the hell is going on?"

The crowd dispersed quickly, leaving Leo, the ref, and the still unconscious man in the ring. Justin should probably leave as well—he wasn't even a member of the gym—but Zack might need a hand. It was the least he could do considering everything Zack had done for him.

Leo pulled his protector off. "Hey, I don't know what happened. I must have landed on a weird angle or something."

"We don't do knockouts in training fights." Zack stuck his finger in Leo's face. "That's your second warning. One more and your membership will be revoked."

Justin wasn't about to climb into the ring, but they were close enough to the side he could easily talk to Zack. "Would you like me to call an ambulance?"

"Yes. Kevin, find out if he has ID here. We'll need his health card for the hospital."

"Sure thing." A younger man took off.

Leo stood over the prone man and smiled. "He'll be okay."

"You landed a late hit." Justin really shouldn't be getting involved in this, but given that this asshole was about to go on a date with Finn, he simply couldn't help himself.

Leo snorted, but kept his eyes on Zack. "The bell rang as I was taking my shot. I couldn't have stopped."

Zack looked ready to kill him. "Justin, would you mind waiting outside for the ambulance once you call it?"

"Certainly." That was a dismissal if he'd ever heard one.

By the time the ambulance arrived, the other fighter had regained consciousness and was talking easily to Zack. He didn't want to go get checked out, but Zack insisted he go with the paramedics. Leo had disappeared, no doubt to go bask in the glow of his tainted victory.

Once the dust had settled and Justin was alone with Zack, the words he'd been holding back rushed from him. "Leo's an asshole."

"Yes, he is." Zack braced his hands on his hips and stared at the locker room. "Apparently his father is some sort of big-name lawyer. I want to make sure if I kick his ass to the curb, that I've done it properly. The last thing we need is a lawsuit."

"You're a private business. Your rules are all that matter."

"And our policy is a *three strikes* one. Though I might have to reconsider that going forward."

Justin wished that Finn had been here to see this. It might have opened his eyes to Leo's faults. "Good luck with him."

"Thanks."

Justin headed upstairs, furious about what had happened. How the hell could he help Finn win this jerk over, and still have a conscience? But Finn was so taken with him, Justin knew anything he'd say that would make Leo look bad would only come across as him being petty. Finn was going to have to come to his own conclusions. Hopefully, he'd do that before he got hurt as well.

Wandering around his pitiful apartment, he tried to mentally get ready for tonight. Normally, he'd have created a script for this, something witty that was sure to win Leo over and make Finn happy. He'd had a few lines in mind back when Finn had mentioned the date, but nothing concrete. Nothing that he'd easily be able to use spur-of-the-moment. That meant he'd have to put his improvisation skills to the test.

The knock on his door had him glance at the clock. Finn was thirty minutes late. "It's open."

Finn stuck his head in. "Hey. Sorry."

"It's fine. I'm not exactly ready for this."

Finn's frown pulled deep lines around his mouth. "I heard chatter downstairs about Leo."

Well, that was one less thing Justin would have to worry about. "I was there and saw it happen."

Finn leaned against the wall. "How close to the bell did the hit land?"

"Close enough that people will say he probably didn't hear it."

"You don't sound convinced."

Justin let out a huff. He needed to choose his words carefully. "I like to consider myself good at reading body language. I've spent a lot of time in boardrooms, involved in some serious deal making. Leo looked like a man who saw an opening and wasn't about to let it go."

"But there's a chance he didn't hear the bell." Finn groaned. "Shit."

"Do you want to cancel?" Justin stood and walked over to Finn. "You don't have to do this. He isn't . . . the only man out there for you." *We can have dinner, watch a movie.*

Every twitch of the internal battle Finn was waging showed on his face. "I haven't been on a date, a real date, in so long I can't remember when it was. I'm tired of being alone."

Justin ran his tongue along his lips. "You can do online dating. Get to know the person that way."

"Tried that. Every time we got to the meeting-in-person stage, I couldn't force myself to go." Finn dropped his chin to his chest. "No, I need to go tonight. I need to see this through to the end. If I don't, I'll always second-guess myself. Always regret not showing up."

You're better than him. "Then you better show me how to use this equipment."

CHAPTER FIFTEEN

"Testing, testing. Let me know if you can hear me."

Justin's voice filled Finn's ear in a way that felt completely foreign and a bit off-putting. It was as though his conscience had been given a voice and now directed his every move. He was currently standing in the bathroom of the Pear Tree restaurant, adjusting his shirt and trying not to play with the earbud. "I hear you."

"And I hear you. Well, this will be an interesting learning experience if nothing else."

It would also be difficult. With one ear essentially blocked, Finn would have to focus extra hard to be able to hear Leo. The restaurant wasn't busy this early in the evening, but there was enough ambient noise to concern him.

A man came into the bathroom and went immediately for the stall. The bang of the door wasn't louder than normal, but Justin made a soft noise of surprise. "Your mic is really good. I take it you're no longer alone?"

Instead of answering, Finn turned the water on and washed his hands.

"You can't say a word, and I can yammer on in your ear." Justin's chuckle sent a shiver through him. "This is going to be the most fun I've had in months."

Reaching into his pocket, Finn pulled out his cell phone. "Hello? Hey. Yes, I'm here." He then left the bathroom. "With my phone, no one will think I'm talking to myself."

"They probably wouldn't at any rate. Enough people have these things with their phones, people would make assumptions."

God, Finn hated how freaking logical Justin could be. "I'll feel better, how's that?"

"Fair enough. Now, down to business. Is he there yet?"

Finn retook his seat at the still-empty table. "No." His nerves had him fumbling with his cutlery and tapping out a beat on the table with his fingers.

"It's only been ten minutes. He doesn't strike me as necessarily the prompt type."

"You don't like him, do you?" Justin had never come right out and said it, but it was clear from his tone and careful words whenever the topic of Leo came up.

"It's not my place to pass judgment. I'm here helping you as a friend."

Finn smiled. "We are friends, aren't we? Like, really honestly friends, not just two guys doing something crazy together."

"Of course. Two lonely men spending time determining how to land a third as a potential mate. As friends do."

The laugh that popped from him was unexpected. "You're funny."

"Never been accused of that before."

It was then that Finn glanced up to see Leo enter the restaurant.

"Based on the sudden gasp, I imagine Leo just arrived?"

Finn jumped to his feet, his burst of nerves making it impossible to sit still. "Hey."

Leo had on a tight pair of black jeans, and a shirt that showed off his biceps. "There's my guy. Good to see you." He stuck out his hand and grinned. "Looking good . . ."

"Finn."

Justin groaned. "He forgot your name? Wonderful start."

Finn clenched his teeth, biting back a response. Leo's hand was warm and big, but he squeezed Finn's far harder than necessary. Finn managed to conceal his wince. "I wasn't sure you were coming."

"Why?"

"Ah, we were supposed to meet at five."

"We were?" Leo glanced at his phone. "Dude, it's only twenty after. You know what traffic is like."

Justin snorted. "I would think he knows exactly how long it takes him to get here."

Leo sat down and flagged the waiter over. "Hey, beautiful. Can we get a couple of beers here? I saw you had a local dark on tap. Those will do." He turned back to Finn and smiled. "You're okay with beer, right?"

"Sure." Finn was more of a wine person, but anything would be helpful now that the moment of truth was at hand.

Leo turned in his chair so his arm draped across the back and his ankle was braced on his opposite knee. "Mr. Finn. You're quite the good-looking man. Why haven't we gone out for drinks before?"

Okay, this is the conversation starter. He threw you a fucking softball. Say something! "Ah . . . not sure."

Finn's heart was pounding so hard, the sound of it was echoing around the ear piece. His palms were full-on damp now and for the slightest of moments, his vision darkened. Shit, he wasn't going to be able to do this. Who the hell did he think he was, going out on a date with someone like Leo? God, Leo hadn't even remembered Finn's name; he was that unmemorable.

As his panic reached a crescendo, a soft voice in his ear came to his rescue. "Finn, breathe."

He took in a breath, held it for a count of three, before letting it go.

"Good, now I want you to smile at Leo." Finn smiled. "Give your head a little shake." He did. "Excellent, now say this . . ."

Justin's words drove Finn's voice. "I'm sorry. I'm nervous. I've been admiring you at the gym for so long, it's hard to believe I'm sitting here with you."

It was clearly the right thing to say. Leo's entire demeanor changed. He dropped his foot to the floor, and leaned his forearms on the edge of the table. "Well, aren't you the smooth talker? I have to admit I only knew your face because you trained with Eli."

Justin clicked his tongue. "Say, 'I bet you'd love to get into the ring with him for real. Not one of those training matches.'"

Finn took a sip of water. "I bet you'd love to, ah, get into the ring with him. For real. Not just . . . ah, a training match."

"Good job." Justin's praise helped ease Finn's building tension as Leo started to respond. "When he's talking, make sure to maintain eye contact as long as you're able. You have a tendency to look anywhere but the person you're speaking to."

That turned out to be far more difficult than Finn had expected. Thankfully, Leo was talking away, apparently oblivious to Finn's struggles.

"I've been fascinated with him for years. Dude is brutal in the ring. It's a fucking shame he retired when he did. Sure, he's gay, but that shouldn't have mattered. He would have kicked Caulfield's ass, then moved on to win a title, but he's the reason I got a membership at the gym in the first place. I study him, make notes, but he only let me spar with him once a few weeks ago, and he kicked my ass. I think he realized how good I am and got nervous. Put me down before I could embarrass him."

This time, Finn didn't need Justin's prompting. "Why haven't you signed on to train with him?"

It was strange how quickly Leo's expression changed. For the briefest of seconds, the laid-back man was gone and, in his place, was someone filled with rage. "He said no."

"Eli is only one man, and probably has to turn down clients all the time." The only reason Finn had been able to sign on with him was because of his friendship with Devan. "I'm sure he'll have an opening soon."

"That's what I don't understand." Leo leaned in so his head was quite low, appearing to hover above the table. "He had an opening. He simply didn't want to work with me."

Justin's sudden voice in his ear made Finn jump. "Be careful here. There's something not right."

Leo smiled and leaned back, appearing relaxed once more. "I know it won't take long for him to appreciate what I can offer as a client and he'll change his mind."

"There are other really good trainers at Ringside."

Leo snorted. "He's the only one good enough there to take me on. Shit, I knocked some guy out today. Soon, they'll be saying that I'm too hard on people, and no one *but* Eli will be allowed to fight me."

"We need to change the topic." There was a panicked note in Justin's voice. "Ask him if he's seen any good movies recently."

"Ah, yeah. Cool. Have you seen any—"

"I have an idea." Leo slapped the table. "You train with Eli three times a week, right?"

"Yeah."

"I should get in the ring with *you*."

The waiter chose that moment to come over with their beers and give them menus. "Our special tonight is a lamb burger with our house-made potato chips. We also have salmon with maple glaze on a bed of—"

"I'll have the burger." Leo didn't even look at him. "You?"

"Finn, you should get out of there. Cut the date short. I don't like where this is—"

"I'll have the same." Finn smiled at the waiter and hoped he wasn't too put out with Leo. "Thanks."

Leo waited for him to leave before he turned around and checked out his ass. "Fucking sweet."

Justin cleared his throat, which brought Finn's attention back to him. "Try the movie question again."

"Ah, cool. So, movies?"

"Don't watch them. I train at the gym, go to work, and party." This time when he looked at Finn, his gaze traveled down Finn's body. "I don't know why I hadn't noticed you before now. You're pretty fucking hot yourself."

The blush heated Finn's skin and set his heart pounding once more. "Thanks."

"You're not much of a talker, are you?"

"No. Not really."

"I like that too. My ex told me I like to run my mouth off too much, but he was a prude who didn't know how to have fun." Leo picked up his beer and swallowed half of it down. "I bet you would be a lot of fun."

Justin growled. "This guy is . . . Okay, you need to say something. I can't help you with this one."

Finn was barely aware of Justin's voice then. All he could focus on was the picture of him and Leo rolling around on a bed, naked. "I like fun."

"How about this?" Leo scooted his chair closer to the table. "You and I get into the ring and have a go. If you win, I'll take you out for a night on the town that you won't forget." He licked the rim of the beer glass and winked. "If I win, you need to put in a good word with Eli for me."

"I can do that."

Justin muttered something off mic Finn couldn't quite hear before coming back. "Finn, be careful. I don't like where this is going."

Leo's expression became unreadable. "And you'll even give me one of your training spots."

"I . . . Pardon?"

Leo shrugged. "It's only fair. If I can kick your ass, and you're Eli's best student, then that means the only other person who can take me is him. I deserve the chance to prove myself."

"Whatever you do, don't agree to this." Justin must have been moving around, because he was slightly out of breath. "Put him off, but don't say yes."

"I'll think about it." Finn got to his feet. "Sorry, I need to go to the bathroom."

Leo waved him away. "I'll be here, sexy."

Finn's legs shook as he strode as quickly as he could to the bathroom. Rather than go into the men's room, he stepped into the single-user stall and locked the door. "I'm alone."

"Good." Finn couldn't be sure, but Justin sounded relieved. "Are you okay?"

"I . . . I don't know. I think so." Finn leaned against the door. "This isn't going as I'd expected."

"Leave. You're under no obligation to stay there."

"I have to at least get my meal. It'll look weird if I take off now. I don't know why—" He snapped his mouth shut.

After a moment, Justin spoke again. "Why what?"

Standing all alone in a bathroom, a friend on a microphone in his ear, and the man of his dreams somewhere out behind him, Finn wanted to cry. "I just want to be normal."

Justin didn't say anything.

"You still there? I can't go back out there alone."

"I'm here. And yes you can. You're the one doing all of this. You're amazing and I'm proud of you."

Justin's words should have made everything right in Finn's mind. Finn *was* the one doing this. While Justin had certainly been helpful,

Finn was the one saying the words, was the one who had been able to look Leo in the eye as he spoke. And yet, it was still difficult to breathe. "Thank you."

By the time Finn made it back to the table, their meal had arrived. Leo was holding his burger, a few bites already gone. "It smelled too good. I couldn't wait."

"That's fine." Finn ignored Justin's groan. "Any good?"

"It's passable. I'm picky when it comes to lamb, but I'm sure you'll love it."

Leo was right about that. The first bit of the burger sent a burst of juice into his mouth and drew a moan from him. "So good."

Justin sighed. "I should have taken you up on that offer to feed me before your date. Now I'm going to have to sit here and listen to you drool over your meal." Then there was a rustle in Finn's ear. "Oh yes, that will do nicely."

"What will do?" Finn took another bite, sighing once again.

Finn hadn't realized he'd spoken the question aloud until Leo stopped eating and stared at him. "What do you mean?"

The bite he'd been swallowing got caught in his throat, and Finn started to cough. Justin chuckled. "Just say, 'I meant that will do.'"

When he was able to suck in air, Finn waved his hands around. *Distraction!* "I meant, 'that will do.' The lamb."

"Ah." Leo shrugged. "I thought you were going all weird on me there for a moment."

The rest of the dinner conversation was easier. Justin continued to prompt him, and for his part, Leo did most of the talking. Finn felt as though he were participating in some weird version of the children's game Telephone. The only difference was, he was focused on listening to Justin's comments on what Finn would go on about.

"Ask him where his favorite place to vacation is."

"Cancun! They have the best fucking tequila, and I've ended up in a few orgies there."

Justin laughed. "Tell him having sex with an empty bottle while tonguing a banana doesn't count as an orgy."

Finn had to bite his tongue hard to stop from laughing. Leo was oblivious, still going on about his escapades.

When Leo started to slow down, Justin would prompt again.

"Ask him about where he went to school."

"Ask him what kind of car he drives."

"Ask him about his workout routine. That should keep him going for a while."

It did. In fact, Leo talked for so long, their waiter had refilled their drink order three times and the tables around them had changed occupants, who were now eating dessert themselves, by the time he finished.

With their coffees almost done, Leo was still going on about whatever question Finn had last asked, when Justin chirped up again. "You know, had I realized how much he likes to talk about himself, I could have simply sent you with crib notes. Though this way, I at least get some entertainment. I also demand a piece of that cheesecake you're having. The noises you're making as you eat it are obscene."

Leo dropped his fork to the plate. "I'm stuffed."

"Me too." Thankfully, the amount of food Finn had consumed had helped counter the amount of alcohol he'd had.

"Shit, it's after seven. I need to get out of here." Leo stood and threw several bills on the table. "I had a good time tonight. You're more fun than I thought."

"Thanks." Though it didn't feel like much of a compliment.

"Don't forget our little wager. Maybe next time you're at the gym we can meet up in the ring. It would be good."

Before Finn could say a word, Leo came around to his side of the table, leaned down, and kissed him.

Everything Finn had been thinking *poof*ed in a blink, leaving him a blank vessel. There was nothing that could have prepared him for the overwhelming sensation of being kissed by Leo Hayes in the middle of a restaurant.

Leo pulled back, giving him a wink. "See you soon." And then, he was gone.

"Finn? Are you still there? *Finn?*"

"I'm here." Finn didn't even bother to pull his phone out, no longer caring if anyone noticed he was having a conversation with himself.

"What happened?"

"He kissed me."

"He what?"

"Kissed me. And then he left."

"He *what*?" Justin's voice was loud enough, Finn almost took the earbud out. "Did he at least pay the bill?"

"Ah, sort of." After a quick count of the money Leo had left, Finn pulled out his wallet. "He paid for his half. Mostly."

"I promise I will pay you for the entirety of my cheesecake. As long as you bring it to me."

"Deal. I'll be over soon."

Justin packed up the equipment as best as he could, giving up on fitting the bits and pieces into the correct spots. No doubt Finn would have a better idea and everything would be righted within moments. Justin currently couldn't be bothered.

Tonight had been hell.

With each flippant remark Leo made, Justin had been ready to march around the corner to the restaurant and punch him. If Finn had been aware of how many times Leo's comments had bordered on offensive, he hadn't shown it. Even his compliments about Finn's skills in the ring had come across as fake, and troubled Justin.

Leo's infatuation with beating Eli in the ring was far too singular for Justin's tastes. It was perfectly obvious to him that Leo was using Finn to get to Eli. And that wouldn't lead to anything good.

Rather than knock, for the first time ever, Finn simply opened the door to Justin's apartment and walked in, holding up a bag. "I have your cheesecake."

"Thank you."

Finn held out a second bag. "And a lamb burger for you too."

Justin's stomach gurgled in appreciation. "You're a blessing." The bag of chips he'd half finished last night had been the only food in his place, and certainly hadn't been satisfying enough. "We seem to have a burger habit."

"Nothing wrong with that."

Finn sat beside him on the couch while Justin dug in to the burger. The smell might have been heavenly, but the taste was to die for. "No wonder you were moaning."

Finn chuckled. "It's one of the best I've had."

Justin should have tried to have some sort of conversation, but the food was far too good and he'd done more than his share of chatting. Finn seemed content enough to watch him eat, which was relaxing in itself. At least Justin didn't have to worry about what was going to happen any longer, not with Finn safe and sound beside him.

"I have money in my wallet for you." But first Justin opened up the bag and peeked at the promised cheesecake. "I don't know if I can eat all this."

Finn leaned closer, his shoulder touched against Justin's briefly. "You say that. You can even think it. But the moment you take your first bite . . ."

Justin scooped the end of the cake and a healthy dollop of the accompanying cream into his mouth and made a noise no grown man should ever make.

". . . and that happens. You'll eat every last crumb." Finn swiped some of the cream with this fingertip. "I should have bought a second one to bring home."

"So good."

Once he'd finished everything, Justin was ready to fall into a food coma. He leaned back against the couch, for once not caring about the spring that poked into his lower back, and sighed. "I'm going to gain twenty pounds living here." Finn was staring at him. "What?"

"You have something . . ." Finn reached out and brushed the food from the corner of Justin's mouth. "There you go." He licked his thumb.

Justin's cock had gone rock-hard. "Thanks."

Finn shifted back. "Leo kissed me."

Thankfully, Justin had only had to listen to that event take place. He might not have survived seeing it in person. "You mentioned."

Finn squirmed in his seat, his gaze dropping to the space between them. "I was wondering . . ."

"Yes?"

"Ah, fuck it."

Justin had rarely been caught off guard in his life. One rare time had been when Grady had announced his fake engagement to Max. Finn leaning in and giving him a gentle but passionate kiss was another.

The taste of mint and chocolate from the meal passed between them, making each lick more delicious than the last. Justin's heart pounded as he leaned against Finn's fit body. The kiss was soft, but insistent, saying all the things Justin knew Finn couldn't vocalize. He cupped the side of Finn's face, deepening the contact between them. Finn sucked on Justin's bottom lip, then he pulled back just far enough to let them both breathe.

"Oh." Finn's voice shook.

"Indeed." This was a far cry from the last time Justin had kissed anyone else.

That had been Grady shortly before his brother's wedding. It had been a personal test, a way to prove to himself once and for all that regardless of how much he'd wanted to be with Grady, they didn't work.

This kiss?

Justin knew Finn felt whatever this thing between them was as well.

Finn's crystal-blue eyes searched him, looking for answers Justin didn't know if he could give him. The only thing he knew for certain was a night of comfort, of pleasure. Justin ran his thumb across Finn's cheek. "Come to bed with me?"

Finn smiled. "Yes."

CHAPTER SIXTEEN

It was the kiss that had done him in. Finn had wanted a repeat of the chaste kiss they'd shared the first time. Tonight, with Justin sitting there, chocolate hugging the corner of his mouth and bliss on his face, Finn had known that if he didn't act, he'd regret it. So for the first time in a long while, Finn had taken a chance.

There had been nothing tentative in that kiss. He'd wanted to inject as much passion as he could, wanted to have Justin imprinted on him in some small way. And what he'd gotten had been a whole lot more than he'd ever thought possible.

Justin was leading Finn into the bedroom, the one place he'd yet to see in the apartment. The room was large, exposed brick and ductwork, giving it a warm, industrial feel. Strong and practical, just like its occupant. There wasn't much in the way of furniture. A queen-sized mattress, minus its box spring, was pressed into the far corner of the room. Justin's suitcase was open against the opposite wall, clothing neatly folded inside, while dress shirts and pants hung from hangers in the open closet.

"You don't have a lot of personal things." It didn't seem right for someone as caring as Justin to have so little.

"They're only things. Never been that attached to stuff." He walked over to the side of his bed and turned to face Finn. "I want you."

Finn shivered. "I want you too."

With the space between them, Finn was able to watch every move Justin made. Justin took his glasses off, folding the arms in and setting them on an upside-down crate he'd obviously been using as a nightstand. "I'm finding it hard to believe that I've only known you a few weeks. It feels longer."

If someone had asked him, Finn would have sworn that he'd known Justin forever. "Do you believe there's someone for everyone in the world? That it's only a matter of time before you find them?"

Justin shook his head. "I'm not that much of a romantic." He began unbuttoning his shirt. "I think that if you're lucky, you'll find someone who fills in some of the blanks in your personality. Not all of them; that would be impossible. But enough that you click. That you work together. The remaining blanks are filled with shared experiences, with common goals and challenges. Those morph into something far greater than the sum of their parts."

When he'd finished speaking, Justin slipped his shirt from his arms and let the cloth fall to the floor. Finn's mouth dried and his cock twitched. The removal of that single piece of clothing felt as though Justin were exposing his soul.

Finn took a breath, then another one before he closed the distance between them. What he wasn't expecting was to see the uncertainty in Justin's eyes. "If you don't want to—"

Justin took him by the wrist and pressed his palm to Justin's crotch. There was no mistaking his erection. "It's not that."

"Then what?"

"I . . ." He shook his head. "Later. It's nothing that will stop this from happening."

Justin then grabbed Finn's shirt and pulled it over his head. It briefly got caught on his head, and they ended up popping a button to get him free. Justin shook his head as Finn smiled. What a pair they were, awkward and slightly broken. Trying to slot their various bits and pieces together.

Justin lightly caressed Finn's chest. "You're far too attractive for your own good."

And yup, there was Finn's blush again. "I could say the same thing about you."

While it might not have Finn's muscle mass, Justin's body was fit, long, and lean. Finn cupped Justin's shoulders with his hands and slowly ran his fingers down along Justin's arms. Goose bumps rose on Justin's skin, and his nipples went hard. The dusting of chest hair was a temptation Finn couldn't resist. He threaded his fingers through the soft brown strands.

Like everything he did, Justin was confident in his moves. He reached for Finn's fly and pulled the zipper until gravity began to help. It took only a moment for Justin to push Finn's pants and briefs to the floor, fully exposing him.

Justin sighed and sank down until his face was lined up with Finn's crotch. "Every inch of you is perfect."

Finn wanted to cover up or run away, but he did neither. "You have too many clothes on."

"I have condoms and lube in my suitcase." As Justin looked up at Finn, his mouth inches from Finn's leaking tip, he stuck out his tongue and licked the underside of the head. "I was optimistic about my tenure here in Toronto."

Finn didn't wait to be told a second time. The necessary items were hiding in the back corner of the suitcase, buried under some pictures and other personal knickknacks. Finn ignored them, got what he needed, and practically ran back to the bed.

Justin hadn't moved. His smile was small, but it made his eyes sparkle. "You're cute."

"I'm horny." Finn grinned and shook his hips so his hard cock swayed. "It's been a long time since he's seen any action."

"Well then, we'll have to make sure that he has some fun." Justin sat back on the bed, his dress pants pulled tight across his own obvious arousal. "Why don't you help me with these?"

Finn tossed the condoms and lube on the bed and crawled up the mattress until he straddled Justin's thighs. He let his gaze shift between Justin's eyes and the erection pressed against the front of Justin's pants. Whether or not his hands were shaking from excitement, arousal, or nerves, Finn wasn't sure, but it certainly made trying to undo the button that held Justin's pants closed more difficult.

Justin cocked an eyebrow. "Need some help?"

"No. I can do it myself." With a flourish, Finn finally worked the button free and pulled down the zipper. "Ta-da!"

Finn leaned over Justin and placed a kiss to his belly, just above the top of his briefs. His skin was warm and still had the faint scent of soap, and Finn kissed and licked his way across Justin's midsection. He wrapped his fingers around the clothing that stood between him and the object of his current desire. But, Finn wasn't in a hurry to race through this encounter. Sure, his cock was hard enough to cause serious bodily harm to someone, but he wanted to savor this moment. Both he and Justin deserved every second of this pleasure. Deserved to feel special.

As slowly as he could, Finn pulled Justin's pants down, his breath catching as Justin's erect cock was finally exposed to him. "God. Look at you."

Justin's eyes were squeezed shut. "If you turn out to be a talker in bed, I will laugh at the irony of the situation."

"I'm not. More into action than words."

It took some maneuvering, but Finn removed the remainder of Justin's clothing until they were both blessedly naked. He slid alongside Justin, needing to feel his warmth pressed against his body. Justin wasn't a passive lover—a man like him wasn't one to simply sit back and let things happen. He leaned in and kissed Finn again, his hands exploring every inch of Finn's body.

Thoughts and feelings became uncontrollable. There was a part of Finn's mind that couldn't quite grasp the idea that he was here, naked in a man's bed, wanting to do nothing more than to press himself as deeply as he could inside him. Finn kissed along the side of Justin's neck, loving the way Justin tried to stop himself from moaning, then failed. Justin continued to run his hands along Finn's chest, brushing his nipples briefly before running his hands down across Finn's abs.

"A desk jockey shouldn't be this in shape." Justin sucked on his earlobe as he ground his cock against Finn's thigh. "No one would guess. You hide yourself too well."

Did he? Yes, that was something he did. It was safer, easier to protect himself from harm doing that. He'd strengthened his body to keep his soul safe. And yet, Justin was right, he never let anyone see it. See him.

Until now.

He rolled Justin onto his back, then slid down to his cock. "Want to taste you."

Justin flung his arm across his eyes. "Fuck."

"Soon."

Finn wasn't experienced in the art of seduction. He was a simple, straightforward man, and his actions reflected that. He ran his tongue along the length of Justin's shaft once, pausing briefly to tease the balls, before moving up to suck the head into his mouth. Justin's hand flew to the back of his head, pressing him in place.

Justin moaned. "Oh God."

Yes, that was what he wanted, this wonderfully put-together man to come apart under his touch. It was a powerful feeling, making another person lose control. Doubly so knowing it was Justin. Finn rose up onto his knees, giving himself access to Justin's balls. He scratched and tugged on them, making sure to flick the underside of Justin's cockhead with his tongue every time he did.

"You're too . . . fucking good . . . at that." Justin moaned loud. "You need to stop. I'm going to come."

Did he want to stop?

Nope.

Finn closed his eyes and doubled his efforts, sucking and teasing at a steadily increasing pace. Justin's body shook beneath him, his muscles doing a silent dance. Justin's hand continued to thread through Finn's hair, stroking him. Justin's stomach muscles flexed, his breathing became labored, and his skin flushed.

"Finn—" Justin choked back a noise that could have been a sob. "Finn."

There was something so deeply raw in that single syllable that Finn's chest tightened as he was overcome with unexpected emotion. He sucked harder, needing to feel Justin's final surrender. Needing to know that it was done by his hands.

"I'm . . . ah. Finn . . ."

The first spurts of come splashed across his tongue, drawing a moan of his own. Finn swallowed every bit he could, for once not minding the bitter taste. He pumped Justin's cock until there was nothing else coming. Only then did he pull back to look fully on the panting, sweaty mess that was Justin.

He was a glorious sight.

When Justin finally opened his brown eyes, Finn saw for the first time a warmth that hadn't been there before. "You're far too good at that."

"It helps to have someone you . . . you like." He cupped Justin's face as he leaned in and kissed him softly.

Justin took advantage and rolled them so he was now on top. "Your turn."

Instead of moving down for a blowjob, Justin reached for the lube and squeezed a generous amount onto his fingers. The next thing Finn knew, Justin had opened a condom and rolled it onto Finn's cock. "Don't move."

He straddled Finn and ever so slowly lowered himself down onto Finn's shaft. It was far harder than Finn had realized it would be not to move, to let Justin work his body down inch by inch, until Finn was fully seated inside him. Only then, once he'd taken a moment to adjust, did Justin smile and began to fuck himself on Finn.

Finn was somewhat certain that he was breathing, partially because he hadn't passed out from lack of oxygen. This couldn't be real, this slice of heaven. This amazing, intelligent man giving himself to Finn.

Justin's body squeezed around Finn's shaft, making all other thoughts flee from his mind. Justin might not have the bulk that Finn did, but he was clearly a man who was used to taking charge of the situation. With his gaze locked on to Finn's, Justin swiveled his hips down, clenching hard before slowly pulling back up. Finn placed his hands on Justin's hips, but more as a way to keep himself grounded.

Justin smiled down at him, just far enough away that Finn couldn't kiss him. "You didn't expect this, did you?"

Finn shook his head, not sure he had control over his voice any longer.

"You want me to talk dirty to you? Want to see if I can make you come with my voice as hard as I know I can make you come with my body?"

Finn groaned, nodding.

Justin leaned down, his lips pressed against Finn's ear. The angle was awkward, and Finn's cock felt dangerously close to slipping out. Justin swirled his tongue around the rim of Finn's ear, before his hot words spilled over him.

"I saw you in the ring, your shirt was off and you were covered in sweat. I wanted to get in there and lick your skin. I wanted to know what you tasted like. I wanted to feel you pound into my body. My cock trapped between us. I wanted you to jerk me off while you fucked my ass, then lick the come from my skin."

"Jesus." Finn growled before using his advantage to flip them both. "Fuck."

He couldn't hold back. Gone was the quiet reservation that ruled his life, and in its place, an explosion of uncontrolled need. He closed his eyes and fucked into Justin, reaching between them to grab hold of Justin's cock. He jerked Justin's shaft in time with his thrusts until his orgasm ripped through his body. The sudden strength that had claimed him only moments ago vanished, leaving Finn an exhausted, panting mess.

After a minute, he lifted his head and looked into Justin's smirking face. "You suck."

Then, the most magical thing in the world happened—Justin laughed.

Finn pulled out from Justin's body, holding the condom so it wouldn't slip from his softened shaft. "What are you laughing at?"

Justin shook his head, his smile still firmly fixed in place. "That took far less time than I'd assumed it would."

"Yeah, well, it's been a while." Finn leaned in and kissed Justin's forehead. "Bathroom?"

"The closed door by the closet."

It only took him a moment to get cleaned up and to get a warm washcloth for Justin. The man staring back at him from the mirror was relaxed, satisfied, and happy. With his smile firmly in place, he padded back to the bedroom. "You should have saved your cheesecake. We could have eaten it now."

Justin had rolled onto his side and pulled the sheets over his body by the time Finn had come back to bed. "I wonder if they deliver."

"I'm sure there's an app we can use to get us food." Finn handed Justin the warm cloth. "Just in case."

"Thanks."

Finn looked away as Justin cleaned himself up, and it was then he noticed his phone indicator was blinking. "Glad I had my phone on mute."

There was a voice mail message that he checked. When the voice on the other end started speaking, Finn thought his world would crumble from the shock of it.

"Hi, Finn, it's Leo. I had a great time tonight. Sorry I had to head out, but I had a meeting with my trainer that I couldn't miss. Like I said, I had a good time. You're not bad company when you're not stumbling over your words. I wanted to know if you might like to go out again. Give me a call."

"What's wrong?" Justin was up, standing naked before him, a hand on Finn's shoulder. "Are you okay?"

"Yeah. Sure."

"Who left the message?"

Finn swallowed. This felt . . . wrong. His stomach bottomed out as he looked at Justin. "Leo. He wants to go on another date."

CHAPTER SEVENTEEN

Justin was all alone in the shower downstairs in Ringside. It was another hour before the place opened, giving him lots of time to collect his thoughts. Of which he had many spinning about in his brain. All of them pertaining to Finn.

He hadn't spoken to Finn since he'd left his apartment Saturday night. It hadn't felt right after he'd found out about Leo's offer of a second date. Not that he knew if Finn had agreed to see him again or not; it wasn't any of Justin's business.

Why he'd given in to his feelings and slept with Finn, Justin still wasn't certain. Weakness? Loneliness? Maybe he'd simply been horny and it had stopped his brain from working. Regardless, it had been a horrible idea to insert himself into Finn's personal life when there was no room for him.

Finn had been beyond upfront and honest about what he wanted from the beginning. And while Justin had become his friend, and maybe a bit more, that didn't give him the right to feel upset when Finn did what he'd set out to do—have a relationship with Leo.

Still, it had pissed him off, the timing of Leo's call. For an hour, Justin had felt like he and Finn had bonded in a way he'd never experienced before. Not even with Grady. It served him right, letting his guard down like that, opening himself up to a possibility of being with someone when he'd *known* it wasn't going to work.

The hot water stung his skin but helped sooth his sore muscles. His mattress sucked, the springs poking into him and making sleep all the more difficult. He also needed to wash his sheets. They still smelled of Finn, sweat, and sex. Not the sort of thing he wanted to be reminded of.

This entire Finn situation needed to be put behind him, and he was doing exactly that. Yesterday, he'd spent most of the day on the phone with contractors, electricians, and the plumber. The apartment was going to get ripped apart this week, which meant he didn't have time for shy nerds and their desire to hook up with a cocky fighter. Justin snapped the shower off and grabbed his towel.

He stepped out into the locker room and came to a screeching halt when he saw Grady sitting on the bench. "Why are you here?"

"And good morning to you too." Grady gave him a once-over, then turned his body around so his back was to Justin. "I wanted to catch you before you went off to do whatever it is Zack has you doing these days."

"So generous." Justin got dressed as quickly as he could, his clothing sticking to his damp skin. "What's going on?"

"I haven't seen you since our run-in at Frantic, and it's not like you're answering my texts. I wanted to make sure that we're still okay."

Justin abandoned his efforts to put his socks on and walked over to stand in front of Grady. "Why wouldn't we be?"

"I don't know. Your boyfriend had a panic attack that I was pretty much the cause of, and then you haven't spoken to me since."

"He's not my boyfriend. Just a regular old friend I was helping out." He didn't even know if they qualified as that anymore. "He's fine, by the way."

"Awesome. I was worried. And for the record, *only friends* don't react the way you did. I honestly thought you were going to hit me for what I did—"

"Have you ever known me to be violent?" He rolled his eyes for good measure.

Grady stood up, shoving his hands deep into his pockets. "Regardless, I came by to apologize."

In all the years they'd known each other, Justin had only been on the receiving end of a Grady apology a handful of times. This one was by far the sincerest in tone. Justin nodded and offered a small smile. "Accepted."

"I'm not used to you being . . ." Grady waved his hands around, before eventually shrugging, "normal. You're just a normal guy, doing normal things, and that's really fucking weird for me."

"It's a fairly new experience for me as well." Instead of his world being the Barnes family home and the Barnes family business, it was now Ringside Gym. He'd traded one city and set of barriers for another. That didn't say much for him. "I was considering taking a few days off to explore the city. I'll have to be out of the apartment once the work starts, and the contractors won't want me constantly underfoot."

"That's a good idea." Grady's megawatt grin was back. "I can't believe you haven't done that yet. How long have you been here?"

"Three weeks tomorrow." It was strange how quickly his world had changed in such a short period of time.

"You should take your *friend* with you." Grady winked. "He seems like a nice guy."

Justin couldn't stop his eyes from rolling. "Don't push."

"What, he is! Max even said. Where did the two of you meet anyway? I hardly ever see you down here."

"The speed dating event." He slipped barefoot into his shoes and gathered his things.

"*What*?" Grady started laughing. "Have you gone on a date with him? Please tell me yes."

Yeah, Justin didn't like the sound of this. "You and Max made another bet."

"After the other night, we sure as shit did." Grady threw his arm around Justin's shoulders and led him out into the hallway. "I said you met at the speed dating thing. He thought you'd met in the gym working out. Max doesn't know you the way I do."

"I don't know if I should be offended or not."

Grady snorted. "Please. And I need to know: date or not? And if yes, have you slept together?"

Justin stepped away from him, needing the space as much as the air. "You know, my personal life isn't for your amusement."

Grady stopped following him and simply stared. "Wow."

"What?" God, Justin really didn't miss this part of Grady's personality. While Justin had been the only person who'd been able to keep Grady mostly in line, Grady had been one of the few people who could get under Justin's skin. He'd dig and poke, question and tease until Justin either lost his temper or walked away. Either way, Grady got what he wanted.

"I'm doing it again." Grady's frown changed his face, making him appear his age, rather than the troubled teen Justin still sometimes saw him as.

"It's fine. I'm used to it."

"But you shouldn't be." Grady looked away, blinking. "Sorry."

Justin turned back and came over to stand in front of him. "We're both adjusting. Our previous relationship wasn't healthy. Part of that was your father's fault for putting me in the position he did. But most of it was on me."

"Come on, don't do that."

"It's true. I'm not an easy person to like. I'm not warm and comforting in my words. I'll never be that man. People need joy and laughter in their lives. They are drawn to light. If I'd been more like that, I wouldn't have driven you away." Or driven Finn away.

"Jesus, Justin." Grady pulled him in for a hug. He didn't let go when Justin tried to move. "You make yourself sound like you're untouchable. Unlovable."

The physical contact soothed the growing pain in Justin's chest. For a moment, he sank against Grady, accepting his touch for what it was. He missed him, missed being a part of a family, no matter how dysfunctional it was. While the Barnes fought like the best of them, they also laughed, ate together, talked, and teased one another.

He had his parents, but the three of them weren't particularly close. Justin had always felt like a third wheel in their lives. He'd been tended after, educated, but wasn't integral to their lives the way most children were.

Justin patted his back as Grady finally let him go. "I'm not a man who inspires love. I wasn't raised in that environment, so it's not something I miss."

"I love you."

Justin stopped and looked hard at him. Those were the words he'd longed to hear from Grady. A lifetime ago, he would have seized upon them, hoping they were romantic. But that wasn't what Grady had meant by them. "You're in love with Max. He's the best thing that could have happened to you."

"Don't be dense. You're smarter than that. I love you. While I yelled and screamed at you when you were obviously doing Father's bidding, a part of me always knew that I needed you. You were there for me after my mother died and brother left for university overseas. You were there for me when my father pushed me away. You were the one who stood by me, no matter what mess I'd gotten myself into. It might have taken me some time to realize it, but you're important to me."

Unshed tears squeezed at his throat, making it difficult to swallow. "I . . . Grady."

"You were my big brother, my father, and my protector. Of course I love you. I want you to be happy. I want you to *let* yourself be happy." Grady wiped away a tear that had spilled onto his cheek. "And if Finn makes you happy, then you need to go out there and get him."

Finn.

A single laugh burst from Justin. "Finn doesn't care for me. He's obsessed with Leo Hayes. That's what I've been doing. Trying to help him get over his shyness so he could go out on a date with Leo. He doesn't want me at all."

"I don't believe that for a second."

"It's true." The sound of the front door being opened was followed by Zack's and Nolan's voices. "I better head upstairs. I have a busy day today, and I still need to check my email." He didn't have a single thing planned, but he wasn't going to sit around wondering what Finn was up to either.

Grady looked past him to where the others were. "Fine. I won't press you on this, but I want you to know that I'm here for you. I'll always be here for you, no matter what."

Justin nodded, not trusting his voice.

"How about I go talk to those two and let you head upstairs?"

"Thanks."

Grady shot him a grin and walked toward the office.

The entire conversation played over and over in Justin's mind as he climbed the too-dark stairs to his place. Grady had considered him a part of his family, someone he cared for. Justin felt the same, though it had taken him a while after his ill-advised kiss with Grady to come to the realization. He'd never imagined that Grady would agree.

He had at least one person in this world who cared for him. That was more than he'd ever thought he'd have—since whatever Grady thought, Justin knew that Finn wasn't meant for him. Maybe he *should* put himself out there, try to find someone who might be interested in a single-minded, slightly irritable man who liked to be right and have the final word in most matters. He was quite the catch!

Justin had gotten to the top step when he heard his cell phone ringing from the apartment. He quickly unlocked the door, raced inside, and snatched it from the kitchen counter. "Hello. Justin McCormick."

"Hello, son."

"Mother?" Justin's legs buckled, and he leaned against the counter. He could count on one hand the number of times she'd called him. Each one of those instances had preceded bad news. "What's wrong?"

"We need to talk."

Finn had been useless at work all morning. His second date with Leo was tonight, and he was in no way ready for it. He'd tried using the conversation techniques Justin had taught him early on, but it wasn't the same. Justin had a way of cutting through Finn's mental chatter, helping him focus on the heart of the problem. He wasn't either self-aware enough or prepared enough to do this on his own.

But the last thing he was going to do was to call Justin and ask for help.

Once he'd left Justin's place Saturday night, he'd felt horrible about the entire situation. They'd had sex—and damn good sex at that—and Finn had then proceeded to fuck it up immediately. He could have left his phone alone and not answered the message, or he could have lied and said it was his parents calling, or his neighbor complaining about King barking again. Justin hadn't deserved to have his date with Leo thrown in his face considering what they'd just finished doing.

If Finn was being honest with himself, it hadn't been until the second time he'd kissed Justin that he'd finally been able to admit to himself that what he felt for Justin was more than simple friendship.

Though it wasn't the same as his obsession with Leo. His feelings were calmer, quieter. Like a trickle of warm water across his skin.

And if he was being really, perfectly, all-the-way honest with himself, Finn had known for a while that his feelings for Justin were maybe, kind of, a bit closer to love.

Even thinking the word made Finn's chest tighten and his palms sweat, which only confirmed it for him. Justin: stern and focused, caring and steadfast—of course, Finn had fallen for him.

Which meant he needed to end things with Leo.

He was heading over to the Pear Tree in two hours to meet with Leo and break things off. Leo was under the impression they were going on their second date, but that was because Leo had barely let him get a word in when Finn had returned his call.

Finn and Justin hadn't known each other long, but when you talk to someone every day for two weeks, they became a part of your life. In Finn's case, having Justin around had filled in a blank he hadn't realized was there. And sure, the sex had been fucking amazing, but his needs were more about having someone in his life who *got* him. Someone who was there for him, and didn't seem to mind his awkwardness. Finn missed Justin when he wasn't around. Like his-soul-ached-for-his-company sort of missed. Not to mention being able to casually caress him, or even the occasional accidental touch. Those little things that let Finn know he wasn't alone.

Well . . . and he totally wanted to sleep with Justin again.

Like whoa.

Finn looked at his computer and noticed that he'd made at least three typos in the line of code he'd been editing. That didn't bode well for the rest of his work over the past hour. Groaning, he dropped his mouse hard onto the keyboard tray and stood up.

His phone rang, offering him a welcome distraction. "Hello?"

"Hi."

"Justin?" Finn sat on the couch. "Are you okay?"

"Not really." There was a pause, and Finn couldn't quite make out what Justin was doing. "I've been speaking with my mother. Apparently, my dad's had a heart attack."

Finn jumped to his feet and grabbed his keys. "I'll be right over."

"No, I don't—"

"Twenty minutes. I'll be there in twenty minutes."

Justin swallowed, his breath catching on a sigh. "Okay."

CHAPTER EIGHTEEN

Finn took the stairs two at a time and didn't even hesitate to open Justin's door. "Are you okay?"

The entire ride over, Finn hadn't been able to help but picture Justin in distress. God, Finn would personally be a hot mess if anything had happened to either of his parents. Being alone and halfway across the country from them would make things a whole lot worse.

Justin was clearly no Finn.

Standing in his kitchen, Justin was pouring cream into his coffee and giving it a stir. "I'm fine."

"Fine? You didn't sound fine." Shutting the door, Finn kicked off his shoes and marched over. *Should I hug him? I don't think he's a hugger. Is he?* He shoved his hands into his pockets. "Do you need me to help you pack? Or get you a plane ticket? I have a friend who does travel stuff on the side and can probably get you a deal."

"I'm not going." Justin held Finn's gaze as he took a sip of his coffee. "My mother only wanted me to know in case I was talking to a friend of the family. It caught me off guard. I'm sorry; I shouldn't have called you."

Finn slowly shook his head. "I don't get what's happening here. Your mom doesn't want you to go out there? What if something happens to your dad? Wouldn't you want to say . . . to be there?"

Placing his mug on the counter, Justin stretched his hand flat on the surface. "I don't have that sort of relationship with my parents. If Mom wanted me to come out, she would have told me to. I don't think it's life-threatening."

"Are you fucking kidding me?" Finn took Justin by the shoulders and squeezed hard. "Do you love your parents?"

"What kind of question is that? Of course I do."

"Is there a reason you're avoiding them? Something they've done or said that makes you uneasy?"

Justin swallowed hard. "No. We're not crazy close, but nothing has happened."

"Then why are you still here?" Finn couldn't imagine listening to a family who told him to stay away, when they were in obvious need. Shy or not, when others needed him, he was somehow able to push past all that and do what needed to be done. "Parents have a way of trying to shelter their children from the worst of life. It doesn't matter if you're ten or thirty-six, they try to keep us from worry."

Justin broke eye contact, but he wrapped his hand around Finn's forearm. They stood like that for several moments. Finn tried to keep his focus on Justin, and not on how hard his heart was pounding from Justin's touch. Finn finally reached up and covered Justin's hand with his. Their fingers briefly entwined before Justin pulled his hand away and cleared his throat.

"As I said, I don't have that sort of relationship with them. I stayed with them for six months before coming out to Toronto, and while I was there, we had supper together a few times; they mostly spoke to one another, and I sat and listened."

"That sounds incredibly lonely." Finn couldn't go a week without getting a call or an email from one or both of his parents. Sure, they might not be perfect, but they loved him and would do anything for him. He couldn't imagine not having that family connection in his life.

"They care for me, but they're not affectionate. Mom gets uncomfortable when she has to deal with a lot of emotion. She wouldn't appreciate me being there."

Finn wasn't surprised to see Justin's cool exterior slip, to see his lip quiver, a torrent of emotions flick across his face. Despite trying to convince people otherwise, Justin clearly cared deeply for the people in his life. Placing a hand on his shoulder, Finn gave it a squeeze. "Did she say that? 'Hey Justin, I know your father's had a major life-threatening event happen, but I'd appreciate it if you'd stay away.' Did those words come from her?"

"No."

Finn tipped Justin's chin up so he was forced to look at Finn again. "Do you want to go?"

It was then the tears started to spill down Justin's cheeks. "Yes."

"Shit." Ignoring his earlier hesitation, Finn pulled him in for a hug. "I'll call my friend, and we'll get you a ticket. First flight to Vancouver we can get you on."

Justin squeezed him hard. "Thank you."

They stood that way for several minutes, two men enjoying the comfort. Finn couldn't stop himself from turning his nose and pressing it to the side of Justin's neck. He smelled good, and Finn did his best to memorize it, knowing it might be a while before Justin would be back. "You don't have to be indestructible all the time. You have people who care for you. Who you can count on."

Justin hugged him tighter. "I'm not used to that."

Finn realized that as much as he needed Justin, he was needed in return. The fledgling feelings of affection exploded in his chest. He wanted to love and care for Justin. Wanted to spend his evenings watching movies with him, and discussing books. He wanted to do everything in his power to make things better for him.

Finally, Finn stepped away, nearly overcome by the strength of his emotions, and took his phone from his pocket. "Let me call my friend; you get some things together."

Justin nodded and headed for the bedroom.

It took a few minutes to work out the details, but they were able to get Justin on a flight that night. "It leaves at six fifteen, and you'll get there at eight fifteen local time. Early enough you shouldn't have any problems getting transportation to wherever your mom is."

Justin only had a small bag with him. "That's perfect. I'll call an Uber so I can head out."

"I'll take you. I have my car here." The longer Finn was here, knowing Justin was going to be away for an indeterminate period of time, the more he wanted to spend as much time as he could with him. "I don't even charge for gas."

"I can't ask you to do that. Not after everything else you've done."

Without waiting, Finn took Justin's bag from him and started out the door. "I'm parked in the lot down the street."

Justin followed him without saying another word. Walking through the gym, Finn was aware they were drawing a few curious glances. He made sure Justin was close beside him, and was fully prepared to run interference if someone approached them for a chat. The last thing Justin needed was to be forced into idle chitchat, or worse, a serious conversation about the apartment development. Outside, the sunny sky contrasted with the emotional storm Finn saw on Justin's face. He had to fight the urge to wrap Justin in another hug. "I'm down this way."

The drive through traffic to Pearson was mostly silent, which for the first time in his life, bothered Finn. On a normal day, he might question if Justin was being as quiet as he was to be respectful of Finn's shortcomings. Today, all Finn wanted was to find the words to draw Justin out of his head, to make him talk about his relationship with his parents, to discuss what he could do to help his father. Words raced through Finn's head, but none of them felt right.

God, why couldn't he talk like a normal person?

Justin gave Finn's thigh a light squeeze when they were pulling onto the airport road. "I'm not used to having someone be there for me, no strings attached."

That little revelation broke Finn's heart. "You better learn to adjust, because you do now."

"I'm starting to realize that."

Finally, after what felt like a lifetime, but in reality, was only forty minutes, they stopped in front of the departure gate drop-off. The line of cars was huge, which meant they weren't going to have long for their goodbyes once they were able to find a spot. Shit, this was all happening too quickly. He'd just gotten used to Justin being around, and now Justin was leaving.

Finn pulled into one of the open stop-and-go spots that was close to Justin's airline. With his heart pounding, he put the car into park and turned in his seat. "There you go. Hey, mind texting me when you get settled? I want to make sure you got there okay. And to know how your dad is doing. And if you need anything else." His hands were sweaty, and he ran them along his pants to try to dry them.

Justin smiled as he leaned over and gave Finn a soft kiss. It was quick, but full of so many emotions, Finn couldn't identify them all. "I will. Thank you again."

"No problem." Finn could only watch as Justin grabbed his bag, got out of the car, and jogged across the road to the terminal.

Justin had kissed him.

Then left. And Finn didn't know when they'd see one another again.

A security guard tapped on his window, indicating that he needed to get moving. With a nod and glance at traffic, he pulled out and headed back home.

Justin's back ached after getting off the flight. His Uber was at least a nice car and got him to the hospital before 9 p.m. It took a bit of asking around, but he finally tracked down his father's room and was surprised to see his mom sitting next to the bed in a chair, sound asleep.

He set his bag against the wall and walked over to stand beside her. He didn't know which one of them looked more ill—his father with an ashen face, body connected to monitors with wires, or his mom. For the first time, they appeared old. Their skin had wrinkles he had never seen previously, and his father's hair was far thinner than he remembered. Dear God, he'd been with them less than a month ago. How could they have aged this much, this quickly? They were always on the go, plotting out their next academic speech or research paper, full of life and talking.

Taking a moment to push down the emotions that threatened to spill from him, Justin schooled his face before gently giving his mother's shoulder a little shake. "Mom?"

"Hmm?"

"Mom, I'm here."

Her eyes opened, and despite the fact she'd been sleeping moments earlier, she now appeared wide-awake. "Justin? Why are you here?"

Hello to you too, Mom. "You called to tell me Dad was in the hospital. I wanted to be here for you."

"There's nothing you can do about it." She sat up, straightened her clothing. It was weird, but she didn't seem able to maintain eye contact with him, something she'd never struggled with in the past.

"Your presence won't change the course of his healing. You didn't need to waste your money flying all the way out here so you could sit in a hospital room with him."

Sometimes he wondered if his mom was too practical for her own good. "I know you might find this hard to believe, but I wanted to be here. I don't care about the money—"

"That attitude is what got you in your current mess."

"Mom." God, she really wasn't making it easy. "I wouldn't have been able to live with myself if I'd stayed in Toronto when you needed me here."

Ignoring the surprise on her face, he went and got another chair and pulled it up opposite her. "How is he doing?"

She cleared her throat as her gaze drifted over to his dad. "The doctor said they'll need to put a stent in. Apparently, your father had a complete block in his artery, but he also has an extra valve. It's what saved his life."

"He always liked to do things differently." Justin took his father's hand and gave it a squeeze. "Does he know you're here?"

"He does. They have him on some strong medicine, and the nurse told me to expect that he'd have large gaps in his memory. He doesn't stay conscious for long when he does come around." There was an expression on her face that Justin hadn't seen in a long time. "I don't know what I'm going to do if anything happens to him." Her voice cracked as she spoke, and she had to clear her throat once again.

It was surreal seeing his mother this emotional, even if she was trying to restrain herself. "We'll get through this. Dad's strong and will be okay. I'll go talk to the doctor the next time he comes in—"

"She."

"The next time *she* comes in and get some more details."

The silence stretched between them, punctuated with the beeping of the monitors. The frantic nature of the trip, the stress of not knowing what he'd find on his arrival, or how his mom would react to his unannounced arrival had had Justin on edge for hours. Now that he was here and there really was nothing he could do at the moment, his body began to protest. "Where's the bathroom?"

"That door. It's shared with the other room, so make sure you lock both sides."

He stood and stretched. "I'll be out in a minute."

"I didn't think you'd come."

Justin froze. "Pardon?"

She was looking down at the blanket that covered his father's legs. "We haven't had the best relationship over the years. With your departure for Toronto and how our conversation went, I honestly didn't think you'd come." Then the last thing he'd ever expected happened—his mother burst into tears.

"God, Mom." Racing around the side of the bed, he wrapped her in a hug. "I'll always come. I'm your son."

"I shouldn't have said I wouldn't help you. You've always been so independent and had everything under control. When I said no to you, you were so angry at me, I didn't know what to think. You never get angry. Your father said to give you time, that you'd come around. Then this happened, and I didn't know what to do. I was losing you both."

He held her close and let her cry out her fears and frustrations. For the first time in his life, Justin questioned everything he thought he'd known about his relationship with his parents. Here was this woman, someone he'd perceived as reserved, someone who had pushed him away and hadn't shown him the least bit of affection, terrified of him not being there.

Justin closed his eyes. "Mom, I'm not leaving you alone. No matter what happens."

"Thank you, baby."

Justin let the wall that held his emotions at bay fall, and silently cried with her.

It was nearly midnight by the time they left the hospital and arrived back at their condo. His mom went immediately to bed, exhausted from the events of the day. Justin went to what used to be his bedroom, but now served as a spare, and stretched out on the bed. He was physically drained, but his mind raced. There was no way he'd be able to fall asleep anytime soon.

He pulled out his phone, surprised to see texts from Zack and Grady. Finn must have mentioned what had happened to them. Justin opened the message from Zack first. *Take all the time you need. I'll run the project until you get back.* Grady's message brought tears to his eyes. *I'm here for you. So is Lincoln. Call him if you need anything while you're out there and it will happen.*

Friends, people who cared for him—despite having had friends in the past, this outpouring of concern struck him differently than anything he'd experienced before now. Zack didn't know him all that well, and yet he'd given Justin a place to live and a job. No one had ever gone out on a limb like that for him before. And with Grady, Justin finally felt as though he was part of his family, was something more than a hired watchdog.

Then there was Finn.

Justin scrolled through his contacts and pulled up Finn's number. It would be three in the morning in Toronto, and there was no chance he'd be awake. Still, he'd promised to check in and he at least owed Finn that. *Back from hospital. Dad is stable, mom is tired. At her house now.*

He pressed Send and then pulled off his shirt. The small *ding* from his phone, made him jump. Finn had answered. *Was worried about u. Glad you made it safe. We've got u covered on this end.*

Justin thumbed the edge of his phone. *Why are you up?*

Wasn't. Left the phone unmuted so I could hear u.

Go to sleep.

Will now. Let me know if I can do anything. Nite.

Good night. Justin's hands shook as he plugged in his phone and took the remainder of his clothing off. Finn had been worried about him. He'd wanted to be woken up, no matter the time, so that he knew Justin was okay. The last few barriers Justin had managed to hold up against Finn came crashing down.

Justin had fallen in love.

Nothing good could come of this.

CHAPTER NINETEEN

Justin had been gone thirteen days, five hours, and a handful of seconds. Finn knew this because he'd set up a timer on his phone to keep track. It was pretty middle school behavior, but Finn had to do something to help keep him focused.

They texted off and on whenever Justin was free. Finn did everything he could to ensure Justin had nothing to worry about while away. He'd taken some vacation time so he could be available to the contractors who were in the process of gutting Justin's kitchen. Given that Justin wasn't here and wouldn't be back in the foreseeable future, someone needed to help Zack. Now that he was back at work, Finn didn't have a lot of time, but he came over as much as he could in the evening. If nothing else, King enjoyed running up and down the hallway, barking at the noise.

Once Justin found out what Finn was doing, he made a point of calling a few times a day to make sure everything was being done according to the plan.

"If I come back and find out that they've put some modern chrome in my kitchen, there'll be hell to pay."

"I'm watching them like a hawk."

"Good. How was your date with Leo?"

When Justin had asked Finn that question the first time, he'd been honestly able to answer. *"I canceled given what's happened."*

"You need to reschedule. You've come too far with him, and your small-talk skills, to give up now. Leave my place and go out."

"I will."

The second and third time Justin had asked, it had gotten harder and harder to put him off. Finn no longer had any desire to go out with

Leo, but he wasn't about to get into a long conversation with Justin about why. Justin had enough on his plate making sure his parents were okay, and didn't need the added distraction knowing Finn had *feelings* for him.

When Finn eventually told Justin the truth, he wanted to make sure they were face-to-face. He wanted Justin to be able to see him, touch him, hear how serious he was. Finn wanted to be able to hug and kiss him, fall to his knees and beg, if that was necessary. So that meant keeping up the charade, living his normal routine until Justin returned.

Currently, he was running late for his sparring date with Eli. It had been a week since he'd done anything remotely related to exercise that didn't involve running up and down stairs. Eli, while always willing to be accommodating, had pushed to make sure Finn didn't bail on him again. *"You're stressed and need a release valve. So, show up."*

Which meant the fates were against him. A traffic accident resulted in a reroute and slow down, making Finn fifteen minutes later than he'd intended. Then the contractor grabbed him the moment he walked in, dragging him upstairs.

"I'm sorry." He told Eli as he finally climbed into the ring and immediately began stretching. "They had a problem upstairs with the electrical panel, and I had to wait until the electrician showed. Then another contractor brought up the wrong cabinet doors, and I knew Justin would freak if they installed them, even temporarily, so I had to get after them about that. But I'm here now and sorry."

Eli eyes widened.

"What?"

"I think that's the most you've said to me at any one time. Ever."

"Was it? I . . . Sorry. I was rambling."

"*Finn* and *rambling* are two words that have never existed in the same sentence before."

"I'm not *that* quiet."

"A month ago, you barely said five words to me when we sparred. Now, you're up there talking to contractors and relaying demands from Justin about doors." Eli grinned. "That's awesome."

Finn felt the blush wash across his face. "I guess."

"Don't get all shy on me now. I like this new Finn." Eli picked up a head guard from the canvas and tossed it to him. "Now put this on and let's see if you've forgotten how to fight."

Eli gave him a few warm-up moves, but it didn't take long for the two of them to really get into it. It had been far too long since Finn had blown off some steam, and it immediately relieved the mental stress he'd been living under for the past two weeks. Not that they ever went at it too aggressively in the ring, but Eli never went easy on him either.

"Way to go, Finn!"

Finn looked down to see Leo leaning against the post in the middle of the gym. It was enough of a distraction that Finn dropped his guard for a moment and earned a left hook to his head.

"Shit." He gave himself a shake. "Missed that one."

"You're not paying attention." Eli's gaze flicked to where Leo stood. "Not the man I thought would turn your head."

"What do you mean?" Finn snapped a kick that connected with Eli's chest, sending him back a few inches.

"I though you and Justin were an item." Eli blocked his next three punches easily. "That one's an asshole."

"We're not an item. Well, not yet. I mean, I'd like to be. Maybe." Finn took a swing at Eli. "Can we just spar?"

Finn lunged at Eli, and they landed on the canvas. They grappled for several seconds before Eli got him in a hold and Finn had to tap out. Eli rolled off him and held out his hand to help Finn up. "Next lesson, we're going to work on how you can prevent yourself from getting into holds like that."

"Yeah, getting broken in two isn't my idea of fun."

Someone started clapping. Leo now stood at the side of the ring, smiling up at him. "You're better than I remember you being. I'd like to have a go at you in there one day." The way he emphasized *have a go at you* made it sound far dirtier than Leo likely intended. Possibly.

"Yeah, maybe."

Leo's gaze was on Eli as he climbed out of the ring and went over to talk to another member. "What are you working on next?"

"Getting out of holds."

"I'll have to get you to show me once he's taught you. That's how he got me the time I sparred with him."

There was something about the way Leo spoke about Eli that threw Finn off. "Ah, sure."

In a flash, Leo's attention was locked back on to Finn. "So, handsome, you owe me a date."

Leo's bright smile had lost some of its shine in Finn's eyes. Maybe Finn was starting to see the horrible edge that everyone else seemed to. It *was* as though he were seeing Leo for the first time. "Sorry about canceling."

"I don't mind the canceling, so much as I mind being brushed off. Why don't you change whatever plans you've made tonight and I take you out?" Leo let his gaze travel down Finn's body. "Once we've had supper, we can enjoy a bit of dessert."

A month ago, those would have been the sweetest words Finn would have ever heard. A month ago, he wouldn't have been able to get a sentence out, let alone stand still without being overcome with embarrassment.

A month ago, Justin hadn't been a part of his life.

"I'm really sorry, but I don't think I'm up for that." Finn climbed out of the ring, wiping his face down with his towel. "We're not a good fit."

"Of course we're a good fit. You're a decent fighter and I'm a sexy-ass guy." Leo winked. "Come on, one dinner. My treat. We can go back to that place we did before, and I'll get you that burger you liked so much."

Finn bit back a groan and took a breath. He was going to have to choose his words carefully, to be clear about what he wanted. Or, in this case, didn't want. "Ah, I appreciate the offer. But while I enjoyed our first dinner, I don't think . . . No, I don't want a repeat. But thank you for the offer."

His heart was pounding hard by the time he finished his speech. He had looked away as he'd spoken, but now he chanced a glance at Leo as he pulled his gloves off.

Yeah, Leo was pissed.

Leo crossed his arms. "You're saying no. To me."

"Yup. You're cool and . . . ah. Well, I'm just . . . I mean—"

"Shit, you can't even get a fucking sentence out."

Finn's mouth fell open.

Leo snorted. "Fine, I don't care about the date. What I want is to get in the fucking ring with you." He took a step closer, so their noses were only inches apart.

"Not that bet again."

"Yes, the bet. There's no way you're a better fighter than I am. Eli might have shown you some of his moves, but I saw you fight. You're sloppy. I want a chance to prove to Eli that I'm the one he should be training. Not some stammering idiot."

The rise of numbness through Finn's body spread like frost across a window pane in late fall. In a blink, he was back in high school, the butt of jokes, the focus of his peers' jealousy. Every horrible thing that had ever been said to him echoed in his head as he stared at Leo's smirking face.

But there was another voice, a quieter one that managed to cut through the din of self-doubt and self-loathing. It was Justin's voice, calm and reassuring, giving him a nudge toward the direction he should go. *Walk away.*

It was easy to think but hard to do. Seeing the smugness on Leo's face, Finn knew it was the exact right thing. "I need . . . a shower." He nodded at Leo and started toward the locker room.

"I'm not surprised you're a coward."

Finn stopped dead in his tracks and slowly turned back. "Pardon?"

Leo sauntered toward Finn. "You heard me. All that training you've done and you're too scared to get into the ring with me."

"I'm not." Finn had no doubt he'd wipe the floor with Leo if it was a fair fight. The problem being that Leo didn't fight fair.

"Prove it, then. Tomorrow in the ring. Show me how good you are."

Oh, this was stupid. And childish. And the worst idea he could have. He should simply flip Leo off and never talk to him again.

But there was no way he'd be able to let this go. He'd let the bullies of his childhood ruin his confidence, and rob him of his ability to have a conversation. If he didn't stand up for himself now, there was no telling the impact this would have on his future. Never again would he let someone have that kind of power over him.

Finn looked Leo straight in the eye and nodded. "Fine. Tomorrow."

Leo grinned. It wasn't the least bit attractive. "I'll text you the time. Need to make sure there's no one around to get in our way."

"Fine." Finn needed to get out of here before he agreed to anything else stupid. He turned his back on Leo and headed toward the locker room.

A class had just gotten out, so there were more men than usual milling about talking. The noise did little to help calm Finn's nerves. There was only one thing he could think of that would help him right now, and that was to talk to Justin. He opened his locker and fished out his cell phone. Relief washed over him when he saw the message indicator. There, waiting as if Justin knew he'd need it, was a message.

We find out this morning if Dad can get out of the hospital soon. It could be as soon as three days.

Every muscle in Finn's body relaxed. He sat down on the bench and thumbed a response. *Great news! So happy he's doing better.*

Justin's response only took a minute to come through. *They're going to need to make some changes. Dad's recovery will take a while. I might have to stay here longer than anticipated.*

Finn read the words several times; his heart squeezed tight. *Oh?*

Mom's still overwhelmed. We've had a lot of time to talk. I'm surprised at how much she never said to me.

God, he was a completely selfish prick to be jealous of Justin's mom. She and Justin hadn't had the best relationship in the past, and it was amazing that something this positive had come out of his father's heart attack. Besides, Justin owed him nothing, and Finn had very little he could offer.

Another text from Justin flashed. *How are things there? Are you good?*

Right, like Finn could tell him the truth about how he felt. Or about the fight. Justin was far too rational and would no doubt talk him out of it. While Finn wasn't exactly keen to meet Leo in the ring, now that it was set, he needed to see it through. That meant keeping Justin in the dark. *Everything's great. Been keeping an eye on the apartment for you. I think you'll be impressed.*

I knew I could count on you.

It was the least I could do. Oh yeah, way to try to woo him over there, champ.

There was a pause before Justin started typing again. *Have you gone on that date with Leo yet?*

He should probably tell Justin what had happened between him and Leo, but that would lead to a conversation as to why Finn had rejected him. While it might be easier to type what he wanted to say, Finn needed to be face-to-face with Justin. Instead, he did what he was quickly becoming an expert in—deflection.

Not yet. Things . . . haven't worked out.

You deserve to be happy. I have to go. Mom is here.

Wait!

Yes?

Finn didn't want their conversation to end. He didn't want Justin to be away any longer. God, he was becoming as obsessed about Justin as he had been about Leo. That wasn't healthy either. Still, he couldn't do this on his own. *Do you mind if I text you? I mean later. If there's a problem.*

The pause was far longer than he would have liked, but when Justin's reply finally came, it was as though a weight were lifted from Finn. *Of course. I'll keep my phone on me and will check.*

Thank you. The words didn't seem strong enough to convey the true weight of his feelings.

And then, once again, Finn was alone. There was no way to know when Justin would be back. Hell, Finn couldn't be certain that he'd come back at all. It sounded as though he'd worked things out with his parents, which meant he might have more support there, and a greater chance to live his life where he'd originally wanted.

Finn didn't have the words to convince Justin that he could have a life here in Toronto with him. That Finn was maybe, probably in love with him. All he could do was hope Justin would eventually come back.

And if he didn't, then Finn would have to learn how to go on alone.

Justin was pacing the hall outside his father's hospital room. He hadn't been able to sit still since he'd heard from Finn. Something was wrong, he could tell, and knowing that made him antsy. That was a feeling he hadn't experienced since he was a child. He was surprised that Finn could affect him that way halfway across the country. It had been more about what Finn hadn't said than anything he had. The whole time Justin had known him, all Finn had talked about was Leo. That he'd practically tripped over himself to avoid the topic was weird.

So, Justin paced in the hall as he waited, trying to figure out what the hell was going on in Toronto.

The doctor was supposed to be in to give them an update on whether or not his dad would be able to head home in a few days. Given how well he'd recovered from surgery, the chances were fairly good. He'd been on the phone with the support nurse who'd be coming out to check on his parents so his father would have the care he needed and his mom would have extra support.

"Justin?"

With a glance at his phone to see if Finn had texted yet, he shoved it into his pocket and popped into his dad's room. "I'm here."

His father was sitting up in the bed, far more color in his skin than there'd been even a day ago. He was starting to appear more like his old self. *Thank God.* "Can you get me some water? I can't reach."

"Sure." Justin walked over and filled the glass. "Mom should be back soon. She wanted to get a coffee before coming up."

"This time of day I imagine there's a long line." His dad took the water from Justin and smiled. "Thanks."

Justin's phone buzzed, and he peeked at the message from Finn. *Contractor is done for the day. Cupboards are great.*

He looked back at his dad and smiled. "What do you want to do when you get out?"

"Sleep. I swear I haven't been able to rest since they brought me in. These beds are terrible."

"I'm sure we can accommodate that. Mom is going to sleep in the spare room so she won't disturb you."

"Where are you going to sleep?"

"The couch for now. I'm not certain how long I'm going to stay."

His father frowned. "Oh."

"Oh what?"

"I just assumed you were going to stay for a while. I mean, you don't have a job in Toronto that you need to get back to."

"I do have a job." He'd forgotten that he hadn't had the chance to speak to his dad the way he had with his mom since arriving. "I'm leading a small development project. Converting old apartments into high-end rentals."

His father's smile appeared forced. "I'm happy for you."

"You don't look happy."

"I worry about you."

Justin's phone buzzed again, another message from Finn. *I've been spending too much time at the gym. Feels weird being in your place. I feel like a stalker.*

Justin snorted before thumbing out a response. *I'm terrified.*

I'm home now. Not having a good day. Wish you were here.

Need me to call you?

No. I'll be fine. Just miss you.

"Who's that you're talking to?" His father sat up a bit straighter and tried to look at his screen.

"A friend." Justin flipped the phone over on the bed to hide the screen. "Sorry."

"Don't be. It's nice to see you smile."

The shock that bolted through him was nearly as much of a surprise as his father's words. "I wasn't smiling."

"Yes, you were." His dad leaned back, giving Justin one of those assessing professor stares that used to drive him nuts as a kid. "Tell me about him. I assume it's a him."

"He is." Justin shifted awkwardly. "He's only a friend. I volunteered at a speed dating event when I first arrived in Toronto. A charity thing. He was trying to get a date and failing miserably." It didn't take long for him to relay the story of how he'd met Finn and what he'd thought of him in those first few minutes. "He's very smart but lacks confidence. I've been coaching him on how to manage in social situations."

"So, he's gay."

"Yes." Justin frowned. "Though I don't see what that has to do with anything. It's not like he's interested in me. His intent has been to win over Leo."

His phone buzzed, then again. No doubt additional messages from Finn.

"Aren't you going to check that?" His father cocked his eyebrow and smirked. "Finn needs you."

"He'll live."

"No doubt. But I can see you twitching from here." Another two buzzes from Justin's phone. "I don't mind."

Justin managed to wait another few seconds before growling and picking up his phone. The litany of messages grew more frantic.

I'm sorry.

I know you're with your parents. I didn't want to tell you. But now I'm freaking out.

Justin?

You must be busy. Sorry. I'll leave you alone.

Apparently, I can't even manage that. Okay, don't be mad.

Leo wanted to go on a date. But I said no.

Then he challenged me to a fight.

And I said yes.

I don't know why I said yes.

Leo just texted me the time for the fight.

Okay, I can do this. It's got to be easier than talking to him. Right?

Right. I *can* do this.

I'm going offline to sleep. I know you're too busy to talk so I'll let you know how I made out when it's done.

Night.

"Shit." Justin got to his feet and looked at his dad, who was now frowning. "I need to give him a call. I'll be right back."

His father waved him away. "Go."

Stepping out into the hall, Justin hit the speed dial for Finn. It rang through to voice mail. He hung up and tried again, but got the same result. "You've reached Finn. Leave a message."

"Damn it." Justin thumbed out a quick text. *Don't fight him. Finn?*

Now that things had been set in motion, Justin had no doubt Finn would see them through, even if that meant fighting with someone who played dirty. He should call Grady and have him try to put a stop to everything. He'd be able to tell Zack, who would . . . do what? It was a boxing gym. People went there to fight one another. Finn had agreed to the match, and until Leo did something dirty, he was well within his right to get in the ring with whomever he chose.

If Justin wanted to stop the fight, then he was going to have to go to Toronto and do it himself.

When he turned around, he was shocked to see that his mom had returned and was sitting beside his dad. She sipped her coffee and gave him an odd look. "What's wrong?"

While things were better between them, he didn't think she'd fully appreciate his need to go stop Finn from fighting Leo. "A friend of mine is about to do a stupid thing. It caught me off guard. He has a surprising tendency to do that to me."

His dad took the coffee cup from his mom's hand, ignoring her protests as he took a sip. "And he makes Justin smile."

"Really?" His mom took the cup back. "Why haven't we heard about this young man before now?"

"As I explained to Dad, he's only a friend."

She shook her head. "Are you sure about that? Because it sounds like it's more than friendship. I do believe you might have feelings for this young man."

Justin wasn't a fool, he knew that he'd been quietly falling in love with Finn for a while now. But it was one matter to have those thoughts bouncing around in one's head, and quite another to potentially say them aloud. That was when they became a living thing, a beast that had a tendency to take on a life of its own. That was normally when his relationships went wrong, leaving Justin a broken mess.

"I care for him. As a friend." Not exactly a lie, but a few steps away from the truth.

His parents shared a look, before his mother shook her head. "You seem to think I can't tell when you're lying. That's fine if you're not willing to admit it. You might not be ready. But if you change your mind, or if the situation becomes different, please know that we'd like to meet him. It's been a long time since I've seen you happy, and I fully intend to thank him for making that possible."

Justin stared at them, the words that he often relied on to get him out of sticky messes suddenly abandoning him. His father coughed and groaned. "I think those pain meds they so kindly gave me are wearing off."

"I'll get the nurse." Justin was out the door before they could protest. It only took a few minutes for him to track down the duty nurse and let her know his dad's status. Letting her go in, he took a few moments to walk the hall and collect his thoughts.

Did he love Finn, or was this another Grady situation? Did they have the opportunity to become something more than what they were? Something lasting, that would see them through both good times and bad. Could Finn be the man whom he could open his soul to, whom he could let his guard down around and be simply Justin?

Justin stopped moving and looked into his father's room. "I'm heading to Toronto in the morning."

His parents shared a look, before his mom gave him one of her small smiles. "Someone need saving?"

"You could say that."

Though Justin wasn't exactly sure who.

CHAPTER TWENTY

Justin was beyond exhausted. He'd managed to get a standby ticket for the first flight out to Toronto, but it had been delayed due to severe weather in Vancouver. Far too long was spent sitting on the plane in the stuffy air in uncomfortable seats. That gave him lots of time to think about all the potential horrible things that could happen to Finn if Leo got up to his old tricks. He'd texted Finn, hoping to talk him out of the fight, but he was either unwilling or unable to answer Justin.

Justin really hoped he wasn't too late.

He'd fallen asleep the moment they eventually took off, giving him a brief respite from his worries. There wasn't a whole hell of a lot he could do at thirty thousand feet.

When he'd finally landed and he could turn his cell phone on again, he was immediately inundated with messages from Finn. He alternated between holding his breath, checking the time, and rereading the words.

Dude, where are you? Still in Vancouver?

I hope you're still there.

You're coming here, aren't you? Probably on a plane.

You shouldn't come. I need to do this, and you'll try and talk me out of it.

I'm going to turn my phone off. I need to see this through.

I think I might love you.

Justin swallowed as he read the last text one more time. Finn—quiet, unassuming, yet completely sexy Finn—might love him.

Fat chance of him not showing up now.

It was almost three, and the plane still had to taxi to the hangar. If he could get a cab and traffic wasn't horrific, he *might* make it to the gym in time to stop Finn from doing something completely stupid.

Not that he didn't believe Finn could beat Leo in a fair fight—he'd seen enough of both men in the ring to know Finn could wipe the floor with him—but he didn't trust that Leo would play by the rules, and then he'd be spending more time sitting in a hospital waiting on someone that he cared for.

As much as he'd tried to tell himself as he'd sat waiting on the plane that his feelings for Finn were misguided or the result of simply being lonely and clinging to the first person who paid him attention, Justin knew that it was neither of those. Somehow, over the course of a month, he'd managed to fall in love.

And wasn't that the strangest feeling in the world?

Justin always prided himself on his logic, his intellect. Justin had rolled his eyes constantly at Grady whenever he'd announced that he'd fallen into true love, because Justin had known that it would only last for a few weeks before Grady was on to someone new. When Max had first entered the picture, Justin had assumed Grady would fall into the same pattern, so he'd been surprised when he'd first noticed the differences in Grady's relationship with Max. It had been the little things, the small gestures that had screamed the loudest that this relationship was something special.

It was only now, as the seat belt sign winked off and Justin was finally able to stand, that he realized the power of those small changes.

Yes, he cared for Finn. He might even love him. And if all went well, he'd tell Finn that before Finn got his face beat up on by Leo.

God, I'm a fool.

Finn paced in the locker room, his gaze constantly flicking to the clock. In ten minutes, he was going to step into the ring and fight Leo. A real fight, without Eli's helpful instruction. The last time he'd done something even remotely close to this, he'd been a teen and had had his ass handed to him. All he'd been able to do back then was cover his head and hope for the best. But now, after all his training with Eli, Finn should have the capability to defend himself and others.

Maybe.

God, what the hell have I gotten myself into?

To make matters worse, Zack and Nolan weren't around. They'd been called upstairs to go through some renovation concerns with the contractor, leaving the gym briefly unsupervised. Finn felt as though he were sneaking into his father's office to do something he shouldn't.

Which, he kind of was.

Cheers echoed from out in the main gym, which meant Leo was probably out there pumping up his groupies. Finn couldn't believe that he'd once been one of them, had thought there was anything attractive about Leo whatsoever. Leo had been cruel and dismissive of Finn, and had bulldozed him into agreeing to this match.

Old Finn would have simply given Leo what he'd wanted, would have offered up his spot with Eli to make Leo happy. But new Finn needed to stand up for himself. Even if it meant getting into the ring in front of a crowd, putting himself into the spotlight with no one to help or support him.

Without Justin.

Ah, Justin.

He'd turned off his cell phone, knowing that Justin would have read and no doubt responded to his last texts. Or worse, read and *not* responded to it. Why he'd impulsively told him that he might be in love, Finn didn't have a clue. No doubt, prefight jitters. They clearly turned him into an idiot. It was best not to know Justin's response until after the fight.

Finn had just finished wrapping his hand when Eli stuck his head around the corner. The second his gaze landed on Finn, he marched over, frowning. "You."

"Hey." *Shit, shit, shit.* "What's up?"

"That's my line." He stopped beside Finn and checked over his fist wrappings. "What the actual fuck is going on? I leave my bag here by mistake, and come back to find out that you're fighting Leo. The fuck, man?"

"It's a long story."

"I plan to hear it as soon as this bullshit's over."

"Okay." Finn looked up at his friend, more than a little surprised as Eli unwrapped his hand and redid it properly. "Ah, thanks. Why are you not talking me out of this?"

"You're both members of the gym and can spar with whomever you'd like." Eli narrowed his gaze. "But if I thought for a moment that I could talk you out of it, then I'd tell you every reason why this is a horrible idea."

Listen to Eli, you fool. Instead, Finn let out a slow breath. "I'm doing this."

Eli shook his head. "Then I'm not going to waste my time. I am going to referee this so neither of you gets seriously hurt."

"Leo won't like that."

"Fuck Leo. I have no doubt that this was his fucking brilliant idea to begin with. Unless he wants to get into the ring with me, he damn well better listen."

Probably best not to mention that Leo would likely be happier with that than having to fight Finn. He flexed his hands, testing the wrap and ignoring his pounding heart. "Okay, I'm ready." *I'm so not ready.*

"Good. You might want to brace yourself. There's a big crowd out there. No doubt Leo told more than a few of his friends."

Finn's heart leaped to this throat as he emerged from the locker room and was greeted by a loud cheer from the sizable crowd. "Holy shit."

"Leo's not the only one with a fan base around here." Eli put a comforting hand on his shoulder. "It's fine. Once you get into the ring, you won't even notice them. You'll be focused on Leo and winning. Let's go."

Finn let his gaze slip, since there was no way he'd be able to look any of these people in the eyes. God, he didn't do this; he avoided the limelight at all cost. He wished Justin were here to see this. He wouldn't believe what Finn was about to do, how he was putting himself out there for everyone to see. There'd be no hiding in the shadows. From this day forward, he'd either be known as the man who beat Leo Hayes, or the man who'd had his ass handed to him.

He followed Eli into the ring where Leo was already waiting. Leo shook his head and pointed at Eli. "What the hell are you doing here?"

"Making sure neither of you do something stupid."

Leo's nostrils flared. "We're allowed to spar."

Finn took in the crowd once again. "This is a bit more than that."

"I work best in front of a crowd." Leo shrugged. "You can always back out."

It was strange how clearly Finn heard the unspoken *coward* at the end of his sentence. "Not a chance."

"Enough." Eli looked them over. "If you're doing this, then here are the rules. This is obviously not a proper MMA ring. There are too many opportunities for one of you to get seriously hurt. So, no throws near the sides. No using the ropes to jump on your opponent. No groin shots, knees to the head, biting or pulling of hair. Pretty much, if I see something I don't like, I'm stopping the fight."

Leo snorted. "Just make sure you don't play favorites."

Eli somehow appeared to grow taller. "Let me repeat that. I will stop this fight if I don't like what I see. Neither of you are professionals, and I won't let anyone take things too far. If either of you cross a line, be aware that I'm more than capable of putting you in your place. Do you understand?"

"Yes." Finn's voice was quiet, but he made sure to keep his gaze locked on Leo.

For his part, Leo shifted from staring at Finn, to smiling and winking at the small group of his friends off to the side. "Yeah. Let's do this."

"Finn, put your headgear on." Eli directed them each to opposite corners, before heading over to Leo to check his equipment. That left Finn standing there, looking at the crowd. Leo's groupies were pointing at him, laughing and shaking their heads, as though they already knew the outcome of the fight. Memories of his valedictorian speech flooded his mind, turning his stomach until he thought he might throw up.

Who the hell did he think he was, trying to take on someone like Leo? No matter what Finn tried to do here, he knew Leo and knew that despite Eli's intentions to keep the fight aboveboard, Leo was likely to ignore the rules to win.

Finn's head grew light, and he had to lean back hard against the corner of the ring to stop himself from fainting. He should back out.

Put a stop to this before he got himself hurt. Eli was right: no one worthwhile would think badly of him for doing so. Finn opened his mouth to call Eli over, when a movement off to the side caught his attention.

The front door to the gym had opened and a wide-eyed and panting Justin bolted inside. It took him only a nanosecond to locate Finn. Dropping his bags, he pushed through the crowd and climbed up onto the ring beside him. "What the hell are you doing?"

Finn managed a weak smile. "I'm. . . fighting?"

That earned him an eye roll. "Don't be a smart-ass. I thought you wanted to date him, not beat him up?"

"Not anymore." The anxiety he'd felt moments before started to subside. Knowing Justin was here, that he'd left his family and flown all the way from Vancouver to see him, made his skin tingle. "How's your dad?"

Justin blinked. "He's fine."

"And your mom?"

"She's . . . Stop trying to distract me. I don't want to see you get hurt." Justin reached up and wrapped his hand around Finn's forearm.

Finn swallowed hard. "Eli is here to make sure nothing bad happens."

Justin glanced over at Eli for a moment, before his gaze snapped back to Finn. "Did you mean it?"

There was no pretending that he didn't know what Justin was referring to. "I did. I do."

Justin turned away, but not before Finn saw the tears forming in his eyes. "If you get hurt, I'll be angry at you. Just . . . please don't get hurt."

Eli crossed the ring to Finn. "You okay?"

"He shouldn't be doing this." Justin nearly slipped off the edge of the ring.

Eli cocked an eyebrow as he turned his gaze back to Finn. "Up to you. But if you *are* doing this, I need to check your gear to make sure everything is aboveboard. Wouldn't want to be accused of playing favorites."

Finn looked between Justin and Eli. While a part of him wanted to go with Justin, walk away from the fight, and wrap him in a hug, the greater part of him knew if he didn't see this through, he'd always regret it. He gave Justin one final smile before sticking out his hands. "Leo needs to be taught a lesson."

"You're going to die. Wonderful." Justin climbed back down to the floor.

The second Eli was done his equipment check, Finn turned around to face Justin. "I'm not going to die. I'm going to prove to him and to myself that I'm not a coward. I'm doing this so I know that I don't have to be afraid of everything and can just live my life. And when I'm done, I'm going to take you home and make love to you until you're begging me to let you out of bed."

Justin's mouth had fallen open and the group standing beside the ring began to cheer. Finn blushed when he realized what had happened. "I said that really loud, didn't I?"

Eli clapped him on the shoulder. "Best speech I've ever heard. You ready?"

The tension that had lived so long inside Finn melted away. "Let's do this."

Eli turned to the crowd. "We're going to have three five-minute rounds. We're looking for a submission hold to determine the winner. No knockouts." Eli turned back to the ring. "Ready?"

Leo grinned at Finn and nodded. Finn held his gaze, letting his mind fly through everything Eli had taught him. He nodded. The bell rang, and Leo jumped to the middle of the ring and tried to tackle Finn. It was obvious and clumsy, and Finn was able to slide past him with little effort.

Leo growled. "I see your bitch showed up."

Rage flooded Finn, and without thinking, he took a swing at Leo's side. As he connected, Leo grabbed his forearm and tried to spin him around. Finn used his momentum to keep from getting caught in the hold. "Don't you dare call him that."

"Aww, did I hurt his feelings?" Leo tried a spinning kick, but Finn was able to block it easily.

"You can do it, Finn!" Justin's voice cut through the din of the crowd. "Kick his ass."

Finn couldn't risk looking at Justin, and jerked away from Leo's next swing. "Justin is ten times the man you are."

Leo growled as he landed a side kick to Finn's ribs. "Fuck you."

"Wouldn't touch you with a pole, asshole."

Finn's rage helped him fix on doing exactly what Justin wanted—kicking Leo's ass. They traded blows back and forth until the bell finally rang. Finn kept his focus and ducked a late swing by Leo.

"Hey!" Eli got between them, his anger palpable. "That's your first warning, Leo. I see that again and I'm declaring Finn the winner. Now, get in your corners."

Sweat covered every inch of Finn's body, but so far, he felt good. He'd landed a few blows to Leo's midsection, who was wincing slightly as he wiped his face down with a towel. Finn searched for his own towel, only to have Justin hand it to him. "I had no idea five minutes could be so damn long."

Finn chuckled. "It's not that bad."

"Yes, it is. By my estimation, he connected at least three solid punches to your abdomen and that spiny kick thing to your side. Are you hurt?"

"I'm good." Finn smiled down into Justin's concerned face. "I want to kiss you."

"Then don't get your teeth knocked out."

The bell rang again, and Finn marched out to the middle of the ring. Leo was far less cocky than he'd been in the first round. As he tried to maneuver Finn around the ring, his swings were controlled, and his kicks calculated. As were his verbal barbs.

"Your boyfriend's that prissy asshole who works here. Figures you'd go for someone like that."

Finn stepped back, avoiding another hit. Then he quickly spun around and landed a spinning kick to Leo's shoulder that sent him staggering. "Justin has more class and sex appeal without trying, than you'll have in your life."

It had taken Finn most of the first round to realize Leo had a major tell. Leo would let his right hand drop before he took a step back and attempted a snap kick. The move was sloppy and presented Finn with an opportunity. All he needed to do was to reach out and take it.

The easiest way was to get under Leo's skin.

Finn circled around him, smiling as he went. "All you do is talk and talk, but you never say anything worth listening to. You're not a good fighter, and you're a worse person. Justin's selfless, caring, and one of the best men I know. I'll be lucky if he agrees to date me."

It was then that Finn did risk looking over at Justin. He was standing there, his mouth in a tight line watching Finn. For the briefest of seconds, he smiled and nodded, before a horrified expression crossed his face. That was the moment Leo handed a blow to Finn's chin.

"Finn!" Justin's voice cut through the crowd noise.

But Finn's attention was now locked on Leo. "Lucky shot."

"I'll show you lucky." Leo took another swing.

Finn continued to defend himself, blocking shot after shot. Careful not to get too close, he smiled at Leo. "Totally luck. No wonder Eli won't fight you again. You're not worth his time."

Leo growled before he nearly landed a right hook. "Fucker."

"Nope, I'm a tech guy." Finn landed a push-kick, moving Leo back several inches. "You're an arrogant ass who thinks he's God's gift. You talk too much, and you can't fight to save your life."

Leo let out a shout, as his hand dropped, and stepped back. *There it is!* Finn lunged forward and drove Leo back onto the mat. He heard Leo's breath forced from his lungs, which gave him the precious seconds he needed to wrap Leo up into the hold he and Eli had practiced the week before.

The time ticked off in his head—*three, two, one*—before the bell rang and the crowd erupted into cheers. The next thing Finn knew, Eli was pulling him off Leo and holding his hand up in the air. "Ringside, we have your winner!"

Finn stood there blinking at everyone cheering and broke out into a huge smile. "I did it."

"You did. Congratulations, champ."

Leo jumped to his feet and shoved Finn. "You cheated."

"He did not." Eli got between them and in Leo's face. "And I suggest you back off."

Finn shook his arms out, releasing the tension. "You have a tell. Once I noticed, I was able to take advantage."

Leo dropped a step and drew back his fist. Without thinking, Finn pushed Eli to the side and let the shot connect with the side of his own head. The shock of the blow was absorbed by his headgear, though the impact still rattled his brain.

Eli grabbed Leo by the wrist and spun him around until Leo's hand was pinned behind his back. "And you're done. Let's go, asshole."

The crowd parted as Zack made his way to the ring. "All right, asshole, that was your last chance. Leo, your membership is revoked. Now get your things and get out of here."

Zack and a few other members pushed Leo out of the ring before escorting him to the locker room.

Justin climbed into the ring. "Are you okay?" He helped Finn take off his headgear, then gave him a good looking over. "Shit, you have some bruises forming already."

The energy that had kept him running had finally petered out, leaving Finn utterly exhausted. "I need a shower and a beer."

"Let's go up to my place."

Shit. "Right, we can't do that. They moved on from the kitchen and started tearing apart your bathroom. The place is a mess."

"Fine, we'll go to yours. I'm not going to leave your side until I know everything is okay and that you didn't get seriously hurt."

It took Finn a second to realize something was wrong. "Are you crying?"

Justin opened his mouth, no doubt to protest, but when a tear rolled down his face, he shook his head. "You scared the shit out of me. I thought you were going to get killed."

"Naw, Leo isn't as good as he thinks he is. Plus, Eli wouldn't have let anything happen."

"Please don't do that again. Don't put yourself in harm's way for me."

Ignoring his sweaty body and the curious onlookers, Finn cupped Justin's face and stepped against him. "Not unless I have no other choice. You . . . mean so much to me."

And then he did what he'd wanted to from the moment Justin had burst into the gym, and kissed him long and hard. Their tongues danced as Justin sighed, deepening the contact. All Finn's fears vanished, leaving him with the comfort of knowing that Justin cared for him.

Finn soaked in everything about him and wanted nothing more than to stretch out on his bed with Justin pressed to his side. He wanted to hold him until they fell asleep. He wanted to make love to him when they woke up. Finn wanted to spend every moment of every day with Justin. He blushed once the kiss broke, which was followed by some cheers and a few whistles.

Finally, Finn pulled back far enough to speak. "I think I love you."

Justin's smile had his eyes glowing. "No thinking on my part. I know I love you." He then placed another quick kiss on his lips. "That said, you're quite disgusting. Let's get you home so you can shower and then we can talk."

"Sounds good."

Finn didn't let go of Justin, not even when he was getting dressed and when they were leaving the gym. He kept in contact with some piece of him—he never wanted to let go.

Finn might not have gone to the speed dating event a month ago with the intention of finding love, but life had a funny way of giving you what you needed.

And he needed Justin.

EPILOGUE

One Month Later

Justin rolled across the bed, enjoying the stretch of his muscles as he twisted and turned. King had joined him on the bed at some point, and was currently curled up beside him, snoring. Justin gave him a gentle scratch behind the ear and a few moments later, King wriggled onto his back, looking for a belly rub.

"Silly dog." Justin made sure to pay special attention to the tiny arm pits, rubbing them until King's tongue emerged from the side of his mouth. "Where's Finn? Go find Finn."

King twisted and bolted from the bed, leaving Justin alone to flop back onto the pillow.

The last couple of nights had been far longer than he was used to. The contractors had put the finishing touches on the apartment, and he was ready to unveil the end result to Zack today. It had been a long haul, with more than a few unexpected pitfalls, but everything had turned out better than Justin had hoped. He'd had a real estate agent in yesterday to give him an idea on what they could list each unit at if they were all up to the standard set by their model. If they even got remotely what he'd been quoted, Zack would make back his money and then some in no time.

The smell of frying bacon filled the bedroom air. Finn had gotten into this habit of cooking enormous breakfasts whenever Justin stayed over. It was comforting in a way he'd grown far too accustomed to.

Pulling his discarded T-shirt on, he adjusted his twisted boxers before heading out to the kitchen. "Good morning."

"Shit." Finn pouted as he flipped a pancake. "I was hoping to give you breakfast in bed."

"Blame the bacon. It called to me." Sneaking around the island, he took a piece of the troublesome pork to shove into his mouth, but dropped it instead. "Hot!"

King snatched it before Justin could grab it, and ran over to his bed to enjoy his prize.

Finn chuckled. "That'll teach you."

Since the day of the fight, Justin had spent most of his time with Finn than without. He'd given up trying to remember to bring his overnight bag a few weeks ago, and had taken the radical step of buying some toiletries and hiding them in a corner of Finn's bathroom. It hadn't felt strange at all, using the toothbrush here more than the one back at his apartment.

Finn set a plate in front of him and turned to put coffee in the mug Justin had claimed for his own. "So, today's the big reveal?"

"It is. I'm fairly confident Zack is going to be impressed with the end result." He took a sip of his coffee and moaned. "I'm happy to be able to see this through to the end before I start my new job. Nothing worse than having two bosses with competing agendas."

Justin was anxious to start his new position as a project manager for the contracting company who'd worked on the condo. He'd never have guessed that renovating old buildings would be such an enjoyable prospect.

Finn gave his hand a squeeze. "Zack will love it."

"I know he will. He'll probably also end up kicking me out because I have no doubt that there will be so much interest, he'll need the space."

Finn nodded as his face flushed.

Justin had been around long enough to know when Finn's brain was working overtime. "What?"

Finn shrugged. "Would that be such a bad thing?"

"Well, it would mean I'd need to find a new place to live, so there's that."

Finn turned around and started wiping down the stove. "You wouldn't really have to look *that* hard."

Justin set the mug down and stared at the back of Finn's head. He'd grown to love that head, and everything else that was attached to it. He hadn't thought he'd ever have the opportunity to have this sort of open and honest relationship—not to mention being able to have incredibly hot sex whenever he wanted. They were still working on the whole communication thing, which was why he wasn't sure what Finn was getting at. "What do you mean?"

Finn spun around and took a deep breath. "I mean you've been over here with me almost every night for nearly a month, which is awesome. But it sucks the nights you go back and stay at your place, and I know, yes, you have reasons for that, but I still miss waking up next to you. And King whines when you're not around now, which is super annoying. And like you said, Zack will probably want to sell the place anyway, so why don't you just move in here with me?"

Justin leaned back against the counter. "Pardon?"

Finn dropped the cloth in the sink and stepped against Justin, kissing him hard for a moment. "Move in with me. Please."

The last missing piece from his life slipped silently into place as he relaxed. "Of course I will."

"Thank God." Finn wrapped his arms around Justin and kissed him again.

As things seemed to go between them, they temporarily forgot about the food and made their way back to the bedroom. It took little effort for Finn to strip Justin of what clothing he had on, and stretch him out on the bed. The warmth of Finn's mouth swallowed down Justin's cock, drawing a sigh from him. It felt natural to run his fingers through Finn's hair, touching the man who'd become so precious to him in such a short time.

Justin widened his legs and let Finn press two fingers into his ass. He was still stretched and a bit tender from their lovemaking last night, but Finn always knew when he needed to be gentle, to go slow. Justin let the excitement, the pleasure wash over him. "God, I can't wait to do this every day. Be with you."

Finn moaned around Justin's cock, sending ripples of pleasure through him. He licked up the side of Justin's shaft before getting to his knees. "I want you in me."

A full-body shiver raced through Justin. "Lie back."

With their positions now reversed, Justin took the chance to place kisses on every inch of Finn's skin he could reach. He spent extra time teasing Finn's nipples, loving the sound of his laugher as Finn tried to squirm away. Laughter in bed with a man he loved. How did he get this lucky?

It only took him a minute to stretch Finn with his fingers and use enough lube that there wouldn't be discomfort. They then stretched out together, Justin pressing into him from behind. Hooking his arm around Finn's body, Justin closed his eyes, rested his head on Finn's shoulder, and slowly began to make love to the man who'd stolen his heart.

Finn bucked his hips in a counter thrust that pushed Justin nearly all the way in. Finn then reached down and began to fist his cock, stroking it in near-perfect harmony. "Feels so good."

"I love you." Justin said the words against Finn's skin, licking and nipping the spot beneath his mouth. "I love you and I'm never going to let you go."

Finn craned his head around, and they kissed sloppily. The warmth spread through Justin, his body keyed to every move Finn made. It wouldn't be long now before they both climaxed. Holding Finn as close as he could manage, Justin kissed up the side of his neck and then sucked on his earlobe. "I want to feel you come."

Nodding, Finn started to increase his strokes, his body shaking and twitching. Justin slid his hand down Finn's side, until his fingers brushed Finn's pubic hair. Finn moaned and his eyes shut. "So close."

Justin moved his hand again, this time holding Finn's hip to make sure their thrusts stayed in sync. He, too, closed his eyes and let his senses guide him to the place he most wanted to be. Finn's body squeezed around his cock, and Justin's balls tightened. "Me too."

Sweat covered them both, and the sound of their damp bodies slapping together filled the room. Finn turned his face into the pillow as his muscles twitched uncontrollably. In the next moment he shouted, and Justin pounded into him as hard as he could, given the angle. Only when Finn finally settled, did Justin let himself go. His orgasm filled him with pleasure that even he couldn't adequately describe. Over and over, he thrust into Finn, until the pleasure began to taper off, leaving him a contented sweaty mess.

It was a few minutes later when his softening cock slipped from Finn and forced him to get up and head to the bathroom. He cleaned himself up, before getting a warm cloth for Finn. When he came back to the bedroom, he couldn't help but smile at the sight of the handsome man lying there waiting for him. "For you."

Finn took the cloth and gave himself a quick wipe, before tossing it in the direction of his hamper. "Come here."

Justin didn't need to be told twice. Climbing onto the bed so their positions were reversed from moments ago, Justin cuddled in. "So, this will be a thing that we do every day?"

"Yup."

"Did I ever tell you how cute I thought you were on the night of the speed dating?"

Finn shook his head.

"I did. You'd crashed and burned so often, but you didn't give up. Then you told me about Leo in the kitchenette and rambled on to the point where I wasn't sure if you'd taken a breath. I couldn't believe that you were the same man who'd barely been able to say two words to the men upstairs."

Finn pressed his nose to the side of Justin's neck. "I guess I only needed the right man to give me the type of inspiration to motivate me. You helped me find my voice."

"And you helped me find my purpose."

"I did?" Finn pulled back to better look down at him. "What's your purpose?"

Justin cupped Finn's face. "To love you."

Justin had finally found the place he'd always meant to be.

Explore more of the *Ringside Romance* series:
riptidepublishing.com/titles/universe/ringside-romance

Dear Reader,

Thank you for reading Christine d'Abo's *Losing It*!

We know your time is precious and you have many, many entertainment options, so it means a lot that you've chosen to spend your time reading. We really hope you enjoyed it.

We'd be honored if you'd consider posting a review—good or bad—on sites like **Amazon, Barnes & Noble, Kobo, Goodreads, Twitter, Facebook**, **Tumblr,** and your blog or website. We'd also be honored if you told your friends and family about this book. Word of mouth is a book's lifeblood!

For more information on upcoming releases, author interviews, blog tours, contests, giveaways, and more, please sign up for our weekly, spam-free newsletter and visit us around the web:

Newsletter: tinyurl.com/RiptideSignup
Twitter: twitter.com/RiptideBooks
Facebook: facebook.com/RiptidePublishing
Goodreads: tinyurl.com/RiptideOnGoodreads
Tumblr: riptidepublishing.tumblr.com

Thank you so much for Reading the Rainbow!

RiptidePublishing.com

ABOUT
THE AUTHOR

A romance novelist and short story writer, Christine has over forty publications to her name. She loves to exercise and stops writing just long enough to keep her body in motion too. When she's not pretending to be a ninja in her basement, she's most likely spending time with her family and two dogs.

Find Christine online:

Website: christinedabo.com

Twitter: @Christine_dAbo

Facebook: facebook.com/christine.dabo

Newsletter: christinedabo.com/contact.html#newsletter

BookBub: bookbub.com/profile/christine-d-abo

Enjoy more stories like
Losing It
at RiptidePublishing.com!

Dating Ryan Alback
ISBN: 978-1-62649-537-1

Clickbait
ISBN: 978-1-62649-495-4

Earn Bonus Bucks!
Earn 1 Bonus Buck for each dollar you spend. Find out how at
RiptidePublishing.com/news/bonus-bucks.

Win Free Ebooks for a Year!
Pre-order coming soon titles directly through our site and you'll
receive one entry into a drawing for a chance to win free books for
a year! Get the details at RiptidePublishing.com/contests.